EKA 1

LT.   Loring, Emilie Baker.
           Follow your heart / Emilie Lor-
         ing. -- Boston, Mass. : G.K. Hall,
         1982, c1963.   (Large type edition)
           340 p. ; 24 cm.

EUREKA - HUMBOLDT COUNTY LIBRARY
           "Published in large print"--T.p.
         verso.
           ISBN 0-8161-3418-9 (lg. print)

                                edition.
           1. Large type books.   I. Title.

PS3523.0645F56 1982   813'.52
                                         82-15398
                                         AACR2 MARC
    Library of Congress
    09056   86 0695   © THE BAKER & TAYLOR CO.   3164

FOLLOW YOUR HEART

Also Available in Large Print
by Emilie Loring:

A Key to Many Doors
The Shadow of Suspicion
In Times Like These
Forever and a Day
Throw Wide the Door

FOLLOW YOUR HEART

EMILIE LORING

G. K. HALL &CO.
Boston, Massachusetts
1982

Library of Congress Cataloging in Publication Data

Loring, Emilie Baker.
  Follow your heart.

  "Published in large print"—T.p. verso
  1. Large type books. I. Title.
[PS3523.O645F56 1982]   813'.52   82-15398
ISBN 0-8161-3418-9 (lg. print)

Published in Large Print by arrangement with Little, Brown and Company

Set in 18 pt English Times

British Commonwealth rights courtesy of Robert Hale, Ltd.

The names of all characters in this novel are fictitious. If the name of any living person has been used it is coincidence.

I

"Marry me, Jill. Please marry me."

The girl in a white blouse and short tennis skirt dropped her racket on the lawn beside the long chair in which she had been resting after a strenuous game. The brilliant sun poured down on waves of shining auburn hair, on clear brown eyes and smiling tender lips in a vivid face deeply tanned.

She turned her head, looking in surprise at the earnest young man in the chair under the big, gaily striped umbrella. Chester Bennett's pleasant face was anxious as he returned her look.

"Mapleville is a nice village," he said persuasively. "You like it here, don't you?"

"Yes, but —"

"I could make you happy. I'd try very hard."

A slim tanned hand made a quick pleading

1

gesture. "Chester, you're like a very dear cousin I'm terribly fond of. But . . ."

"But." He said it sadly.

Her heart was stirred by the pain in his face. Since she had come, three years ago, on her father's death, to live with her guardian, his son Chester had been tirelessly kind. They had danced together, played golf and tennis; he had taught her to swim and dive. More important, he had listened with sympathy and understanding while she talked about the father whom she had so deeply loved and whom she so sorely missed.

But it wasn't enough. Seeing how the color had drained out of Chester's face, she felt a pang of pity. Yet pity was no foundation for marriage. Perhaps she wanted too much: a great love and shared interests, a companionship seasoned with laughter and deepened by trust. Someone on whom she could pin her faith as to a star.

"I won't hurry you, Jill. If you'll only say I have a chance." Chester grinned at her. "I'd work and wait for seven years."

She was silent. It hurt her to inflict pain and Chester had given her so much unselfish kindness. And yet — for all her life?

"I want to take care of you," he said. "It's queer. You seem so modern and independent

2

and self-reliant and yet any man would feel as I do. He'd want to protect you."

Jill laughed. "What from? The big bad wolf?"

There was no answering smile on Chester's face. For a moment it looked older, grimmer than she had ever seen it.

"Perhaps," he said soberly.

She lay back in the long chair, head tilted, looking up into the deep blue vault of the sky. The warmth of the sun had brought out the soft fragrance of the velvety green lawn, the aromatic pungency of a carefully clipped hedge. The light poured on brilliantly colored flower beds and was reflected from the big swimming pool at the Clayton estate next door.

From where she sat she could see the arching maples that lined the distant street. Already the green of the leaves had lost its first vivid color of early spring and had darkened.

Summer in all its perfection. The year at its peak. She drew a long breath of sheer rapture and released it slowly. So beautiful a world! So much of wonder that she had never experienced in her twenty brief years. So much ahead! Bright vistas into the unknown that might lead anywhere.

But if she married Chester, kind, patient,

affectionate—even as she thought of it, the broad vistas seemed to narrow to corridors closed in from the bright sky. The sparkling light seemed to grow dim. She wanted—her hand made a groping gesture and dropped on the chair arm. She didn't know what she wanted, she admitted helplessly to herself. But—something more.

Chester Bennett watched with brooding, unhappy eyes the radiant girl's dreaming face. How far she had withdrawn from him!

At last he broke the long silence. "Can you tell me," he asked, "that there is no one else, Jill?"

"There is no one else," she said slowly. "Just a—"

"A what?" For the first time his voice was sharp.

The soft lips curved in a smile. "Just a dream," she said.

"And I don't fit the dream?"

Her silence answered him.

"All right." He got up quickly, looked down at her troubled face, the tears glistening on her long lashes. He smiled. He leaned forward and touched her cheek gently with a finger. "Don't worry about it, dear. And I won't tell Mother and Dad. They love you so much they'll be terribly disappointed. Only, I warn you, I won't give up trying. Okay?"

She brushed away her tears. "Okay," she said gaily. She jumped to her feet. "I must take a shower and change. Then I'm going over to the Institute."

"You spend half your time there. What's the big attraction?"

"It was Dad's dream," she answered simply, "creating the Bellamy Institute of Art for Mapleville. After all, his ancestors lived here for several hundred years, his roots were here. He was the only one of his family to spend most of his life abroad. And his art collection was so fine he wanted it to come home here."

"But what can you do at the Institute?"

Her face was vividly alive as she leaned forward eagerly. "My idea is to plan a more attractive way of exhibiting the paintings and sculpture and those cabinets of jewelry. Right now they are too stiff, too—too institutional. Rows of paintings seem so—stuffy, chilling. Anyhow, the governors said I could try."

Chester laughed in genuine amusement. "What else could they do? After all, it's your money."

"I know. Sometimes it scares me."

"Being the Bellamy heiress, you mean?

5

Most girls would think it was a dream come true."

"But it's such a terrific responsibility, Chester! That money is a kind of trust. I've got to learn to use it wisely, to make it useful."

His eyes followed her as she ran across the lawn to the house. I don't see, he told himself thoughtfully, what more I could have done.

When she had showered, Jill changed to a sleeveless cotton dress of pale yellow, brushed the auburn hair into shining waves, and started out on foot for the Institute. Usually, with her inexhaustible delight in sheer living, she was aware of every bush and flower, every stray dog in her path or bird on the wing, every passer-by. This afternoon, however, she saw nothing, going over Chester's proposal. It troubled her, not only because she was reluctant to inflict pain, but because it had taken her by surprise.

When her father had died three years before, an old friend of his, William Bennett, had been made her guardian. The Bennetts had insisted, warmheartedly, that Gillian Bellamy live with them until she was twenty-one, when she would come into her father's fortune and be independent, legally as well as

6

financially. Although Thomas Bellamy had imposed no restrictions, he had left a letter for his daughter recommending that she continue to rely on the judgment of the three men whom he had appointed governors of the Institute: William Bennett, Abraham Allen and Roger Clayton.

No one, Jill thought, could have been kinder than the Bennetts. William Bennett, short, fat and cheerful, had treated her like a favorite daughter; his wife Maud, a thin, querulous woman, had done her best to make Jill welcome; and from the beginning Chester had been a kindly and affectionate older brother.

As time went on, Jill had become aware, though nothing was said, that the Bennetts hoped she would marry their son, but until this afternoon she had believed that Chester's feeling for her, like hers for him, was merely one of affectionate comradeship.

And now? Jill's winged eyebrows, which lent such enchantment to her face, were drawn together in a puzzled frown. Somehow, she still could not altogether believe that Chester loved her. But why, then, had he asked her to marry him?

Young as she was, she had already received a number of proposals, sometimes from men who were genuinely in love with her; sometimes, she suspected, from men who were more interested in her money than in her. In an odd sort of way, Chester did not seem to fit into either category.

So far, Jill herself had remained heart-free. She enjoyed, as any girl of her age might, her unusual degree of popularity. But no one had stirred her imagination, had seemed more than a pleasant companion. Only rarely did she have moods when she was aware of a deep loneliness, of a sense of incompleteness in her life.

Because she was troubled, she turned instinctively toward the heart of the village and stopped at a rundown house just off the Green, an ugly two-story house that needed a paint job. And yet it was, she realized with gratitude, more of a home than she had ever had, for she had spent most of her life rootless, traveling with her widowed father, sometimes accompanied by governesses, sometimes staying in Switzerland or England for schooling.

The big back yard was shaded by elms, with a hammock swung between them, and a gnarled apple tree. The old-fashioned parlor held a wheezing organ, a horsehair sofa, and a plush-bound family Bible. It was all quaint and ugly, but Jill loved it.

The fresh-faced woman who opened the door for her was frankly middle-aged, with an ample figure covered by a big apron.

"Gillian! Come in, child." She held the girl off with floury hands raised in warning. "Don't come near me or you'll get this all over that pretty dress. I'm making a peach cobbler. Come out in the kitchen."

Jill perched on a high stool while Mrs. Sally Meam, Aunt Sally to half her grateful neighbors, bustled over to set her oven. Then she brought Jill a glass of milk and a plate of soft molasses cookies.

"You're getting too thin," she grumbled, trying in vain to hide her admiration for the girl. "At this rate you'll be a scrawny mess in a few years."

There was amusement and deep affection in the girl's face. This kindly woman, as a volunteer nurse, had twice come to her assistance when she needed help. She had given more than nursing care. She had enveloped the girl in a deep but unobtrusive devotion, had won her confidence and had learned more about her real nature in three days than Maud Bennett had in three years.

"Is that a new recipe?" Jill asked

eagerly when Mrs. Meam had slid the cobbler into the oven.

"Land sake, no! I got this from my mother."

"Why haven't you let me try it?"

Mrs. Meam wiped her hot face and sat down at the kitchen table facing Jill. Absently she reached for a cookie and began to munch it. She shook her head.

"Anyone looking at you," she declared in perplexity, "sitting there as pretty as a picture and seeming as frivolous as a butterfly—well, they'd be surprised, that's all I've got to say. By this time I've taught you all I know about cooking and running a house, and on a small budget, too. You can make your own clothes and do fancy baking and decorate rooms real nice. You know how to shop and you recognize a bargain when you see one. And yet the chances are you'll never have to turn a hand. So why? That's what I can't understand."

Jill rested her chin on her linked hands. "You see, Aunt Sally, I want to be useful. In this troubled world there's so terribly much to be done that there's no place and no excuse for idleness. Most of the girls I went to school with are debutantes or they are training for professions or the arts or planning on business careers. They want to be executives.

10

Important women in their fields. That's all right of course, and I'm proud of them, but —well . . ."

Mrs. Meam looked shrewdly at the lovely face over which a wave of soft color had passed. Character there, she thought. She waited without asking questions, without hurrying the girl.

"Well," Jill went on, "there are plenty of ambitious people. All I want to be successful at is—being a woman. But I want to carry my own weight, to be a good cook and create a pretty house and raise a family of healthy children and make my husband happy and still not be a burden."

"There's not much chance of you being a burden," Mrs. Meam scoffed.

"But I might marry a poor man," Jill pointed out.

"I sometimes wonder, child, if it ever enters your head that you are known as a terrific matrimonial catch. You are not only beautiful but you are going to be very wealthy in another year. Look at the way the newspapers refer to you as 'The Bellamy Heiress.' "

"I could still fall in love with a poor man," Jill said with a laugh. "It's been known to happen."

11

"So long as you steer clear of fortune hunters I guess you'll be all right. But you're too—too instinctively wise about people to be taken in."

Mrs. Meam added slowly, "I hope."

Jill leaned back and laughed in delight.

"Anyhow," the older woman said with a reluctant smile, "there doesn't seem to be much need in the modern world for what you call homemakers."

"Why not?" Jill demanded.

Mrs. Meam snorted in disgust. "Food out of a can and dinners on a piece of cardboard and baking off a shelf. Even someone to decorate your house so's you don't need an idea of your own. You can buy everything nowadays, it seems like."

"Everything but warmth and a sense of belonging and rooms that really express yourself," Jill said. "I guess I'll go on doing it my own way."

Mrs. Meam got up to peer through the glass door of the oven. "I still get a big thrill out of this electric range you gave me. It does everything but talk back." She chuckled. "And it might even do that if I ever gave it a chance." With her eyes on the oven the older woman asked bluntly, "What wrong, child? Something is bothering you."

"It's Chester Bennett." Jill told her about his unexpected proposal that afternoon.

"Hm." Mrs. Meam turned to look at the girl. "Going to take him?"

Jill shook her head.

"Well, that's good!" Mrs. Meam exclaimed in relief. "You could do better and that's a fact."

"Aunt Sally!"

"I'm not saying anything against Chester Bennett. He's a right nice young man. Only too namby-pamby to suit me. Always a dutiful son. No will of his own. Only time I knew him to stand on his own feet was when he refused to work for his father and went to law school instead. But I never did like his mother and that's a fact. A sour-faced, complaining, fretful—"

"Aunt Sally!"

At the indignant protest in the girl's voice, the older woman broke off.

"All right, child. She's done her best for you and I won't say another word. Except one thing. Don't soften and marry Chester because you feel sorry for him. It wouldn't be fair to you—or to him either for that matter. You can't build a marriage on being sorry. Never settle for half a loaf. Marriage is too important for you to accept second best."

13

"Well, that's enough about me," Jill said, trying to speak lightly. "Tell me about you."

"I'm taking it easy these days," Mrs. Meam said. "No one sick in the village. Only one roomer in the house and he's no trouble except he's untidy. Hardly ever lay eyes on him except at meals." She gave Jill a broad smile. "He thinks my meals are something."

Jill gave a soft gurgle of laughter. "I should think he would. Who is he?"

"I don't know anything about him. Usually people talk to me. John Jones doesn't. Don't even know how he earns his living or where he's working, though you'd think in a village this size I could hardly help hearing something about him.

"He's gone all day and he spends most of the evenings in his room. He's pleasant enough—in a long-distance sort of way. Keeps at arm's length. All I've been able to make out from little things he lets drop is that he has lived abroad quite a lot. France, Italy, Greece, Egypt. Nice-looking but queer eyes. See right through you. Never miss a thing. Only man I ever knew who notices what a woman is wearing or if you've moved the furniture."

The oven bell gave a warning ring. Jill looked at her watch and gave a little cry of

14

dismay. She climbed off the chair and ran for the door.

"I'm going to be la-ate," she called over her shoulder.

II

Outside the Meam house Gillian Bellamy turned toward the Green, walking quickly. She should have brought her car. Sooner or later, she'd have to get over her fear of it, start driving again. But not just yet.

A horn tapped a gay tattoo and she turned to smile as she saw the battered old car which stopped beside her with a squeal of protesting brakes. The driver, in shirt sleeves, no hat on his graying hair, was a slight man in his late fifties, his narrow face deeply lined for his age, his eyes shrewd and kindly.

"Hello, Mr. Loomis. How's the *Gazette's* great editor?"

He leaned his arms on the wheel and grinned at her. "A big day," he boasted. "News stories breaking all over the place. The Smiths are the proud parents of a fine bouncing boy. Two small children have been bitten by a dog." He added in an aside, "Served them right, too. Tying a can to his tail."

Jill burst out laughing.

"Someone robbed the Gateses' chicken house. A campaign is being organized by the town fathers to stop hitch-hiking. The pace is getting too much for me, gal."

Jill laughed again. "Which of these stirring stories will get the headline?"

The editor grinned at her companionably. "I guess I'll have to toss a coin for it."

"Look at the bright side," she consoled him. "No news is good news."

"I know that," he said soberly. "In these days of The Bomb, every peaceful day is enough reason for rejoicing. But—"

"But you'd relish a little harmless excitement," Jill suggested.

"Excitement?" He pondered for a moment. "No, not excitement exactly. What I'd really like to see is a little—" he hesitated, groping for words to express his thought—"a little civic responsibility. Here we elect men to office, including our President, and then what do we do? We've done all that's expected of us as good citizens, haven't we? That's the way folks seem to think. So then we sit back, like spectators at a ball game, checking up hits, runs and misses, calling the

17

strikes. Cheering for our party. Booing the opposition."

He shook his head. "It's not good enough, Miss Bellamy. Dang it, he's *our* President. Every blinking one of us ought to be in there pitching with him, getting to know the problems, to understand what's going on. It's our peace that's at stake. It's our future that's threatened. I'd like to see every man, woman and child in Mapleville learning what it is all about. Caring about what is at stake." Loomis grinned. "I'm a tiresome man with a fixed idea, I guess."

"A good idea," Jill said slowly. "Let's talk it over soon and see how I can help. I might be able to organize meetings, perhaps. Get speakers up from New York. Use the Institute in the evenings as a place to hold the gatherings. Do you think it could be done?"

"Gal, when you look like that you can put across any idea. It's a deal."

The car moved on protesting at the clash of gears.

Jill left the dappled shade of the great avenue of arching maples, whose branches seemed to lean toward each other across the road, leaves intertwined like clasped hands. Then, when she had left the restful shade behind, the sun blazed down relentlessly on a

18

treeless street that led to the narrow river, crossed by a rustic footbridge.

This section of Mapleville had never been developed. Nothing had been built on it but a warehouse, which had long since been abandoned. During the three years Jill had lived in Mapleville the building had been empty. It was part of her estate.

Seeing it now, she stopped for the first time to examine it. Across the river was the Institute, a shining building of Vermont marble, built along the lines of ancient Greek temples, its graceful pillars reflected in the still water of the river.

What a pity that this dilapidated old building should mar the landscape that was otherwise so lovely. She considered the possibilities. If it were torn down, a garden might be created here. Why make the interior of the Institute a tribute to beauty while the exterior remained ugly? She would ask the governors about it, arrange to have the warehouse torn down. If they approved, of course. Until she was twenty-one, she could not dispose of her money, beyond a small allowance, without their approval.

She considered the three governors whom her father had selected to manage the Institute, buy the paintings, and supervise his daughter and her fortune. He had chosen each of them for different reasons and after long thought and analysis of their characters and qualifications.

William Bennett was a retired art dealer whom her father had selected because of his knowledge of art.

Abraham Allen, proud to be known as "Honest Abe," was an industrialist who had withdrawn from business to devote his energies to public service for his state. A thin-lipped, unsympathetic man, Jill thought, but so honest it hurt. She had tried hard to like him and failed, though she was aware that the man longed for the popularity he could never achieve. Her father had relied on Abraham Allen's sound business sense and integrity.

Roger Clayton, the third governor, she had never met, but she knew that her father had trusted his broader experience to prevent too rigid an interpretation of his ideas on the part of the other two men. Clayton had been abroad at the time of Thomas Bellamy's death and since then he had been immersed in the details of a big business merger in New York. His work for the Institute had been limited to brief conferences with the other two governors.

Jill glanced at her watch. Four o'clock. She

was going to be late for her appointment. She turned swiftly and a man behind her nearly knocked her down.

"Oops! Sorry." He caught her arms, steadied her, and set her securely on her feet.

He was a tall man with a deeply planed face and stormy eyes sunk deep under heavy brows. Ill-tempered eyebrows, she thought. He wore unpressed slacks and a torn shirt open at the throat. He stood looking at her, a deliberate searching look like—a searchlight, she thought. Then he turned and walked away at a headlong pace.

For a moment Jill stared after him. Of all the boors, she sputtered to herself in annoyance, remembering the eyes that had raked her face, the way the man had practically mowed her down. She frowned. Something odd about that meeting. The path had been empty and suddenly he was there. She hadn't seen him until he nearly walked over her. Where on earth had he come from?

She dismissed the impertinent intruder from her thoughts and started across the little footbridge, her thoughts returning to her project for scrapping the warehouse and making the whole section a thing of beauty. Her imagination soared. Perhaps the footbridge could be improved, too, she thought in mounting excitement over the project. Flowers might be planted in boxes as they were along the Bridge of Flowers on the Mohawk Trail. It was definitely an idea.

She had been running her hand idly along the railing, and now she felt a sharp stab in her finger. A splinter. A—why, a long piece of the railing had broken off, leaving no protection at all. It was a fresh break, almost as though the railing had deliberately been ripped away. Could someone have fallen in the river? With one hand grasping the jagged broken piece of the railing, she leaned over cautiously.

Crack! She jumped, nearly lost her balance, leaped back. A pistol shot? It had struck near her, struck the railing almost beside her hand.

Jill's heart leaped, stopped, rushed on.

Crack! This time the noise and the pain came together. A hot searing pain in her ankle. Agonizing pain. She staggered, lost her balance, and plunged down into the river below.

The water closed over her head, filled her nostrils, her mouth that was opened wide in a scream. She choked, drew water into her lungs, and then the cold shocked her into awareness and she came to the surface,

floundering, gasping.

She drew a deep breath of the sweet, life-giving air and began to swim toward the bank, hampered by shoes and the leather belt around her slim waist. The banks of the little river were steep and rocky, but after slipping, scraping the skin off her legs on the rocks, she pulled herself up and lay panting on the ground.

Hot as the day was, she began to shiver, not only because of the breeze on her wet clothes but because of shock. She forced herself to stand up, swayed dizzily for a moment, and then made her trembling legs carry her across the lawn to the Institute. Her wet shoes slipped on the steps, her muddy hand fumbled with the handle of the big bronze door.

She opened it and stood dripping on the marble floor, her hair plastered to her head, water running down her neck, a puddle forming from the water that streamed off the dress.

"Miss Bellamy!" It was Joe Deakam, an old employee whom her father had hired as a guard because he lived alone and was weary of retirement. He came hastening toward her, his old face shocked.

"Miss Bellamy! What happened?"

Jill's breathing labored in her chest, her knees were shaking. She sank gratefully into the chair he brought for her.

"I fell into the river."

There was an exclamation of horror as William Bennett and Abraham Allen came in together.

"Gillian! My dear, are you hurt?" Bennett bent over her in concern, his usually ruddy face drained of color.

"Fell in!" Allen exclaimed sharply. His cold eyes took in the dripping clothes, the water forming a pool at her feet, the mark on her ankle. In contrast to Bennett's anxiety, his manner was one of stiff disapproval. As though, Jill thought, I had messed up the Institute out of sheer malice.

She tried to control her breathing, to steady her voice. "The railing was broken on the footbridge and someone—at first I thought someone was shooting at me, but—" She stretched out her leg. Bennett saw the torn stocking, the deep scratches, then the mark on her ankle.

"Someone threw rocks at me. To make me fall. To make me drown."

It was said now. The words might have been in neon lights. No taking them back. And Jill was frightened.

Allen's thin lips tightened into a line. "Now, really, Miss Bellamy. Why do you think anyone would do that? Oh, I suppose you mean some children playing near the river. But there's no excuse for calling a child's game an attempt at murder."

"Even so," Bennett said angrily, "that's got to stop. Joe, you go out and take a look around. If you find any kids up to tricks—"

"I'll give them a thrashing they'll remember for a long time," Joe said.

"Wait!" Jill called as the old watchman started out. "Joe won't find any children, Mr. Allen. No child did this."

"Just how do you account for this accident, then, Miss Bellamy?" Allen snapped.

Even in her moment of surging anger at his tone, Jill reflected that it was a pity that a man like Allen, who longed to be liked, never said or did anything without irritating people. His intentions were good but he lacked an understanding heart.

"I don't know how to account for it."

"I'm afraid," Allen said, "your imagination has run away with you." He looked sourly amused.

Jill pushed her dripping hair away from her face. She was beginning to shake. "It's not my imagination, and I don't think there

25

was an accident, Mr Allen. The first time, yes. The second time, perhaps. But a third time? No, I just don't believe it."

"A third time?" Bennett was bewildered.

Jill steadied her voice. "The first time," she said, "was the night I nearly died of gas. The fireplace in my bedroom was turned on but not lighted. The window I had left open was closed sometime while I slept. If it hadn't been for my telephone ringing beside the bed —and it turned out to be a wrong number!— I'd have died."

"But my dear child," Bennett began, aghast. He dropped down on the stone bench that ran along the wall. His heavy body seemed to have collapsed. The flesh of his ruddy face sagged as though he had grown old before her eyes.

"Didn't you know about this?" Allen asked.

"Of course I did," Bennett said. "We sent for a doctor and Mrs. Meam that night. But I thought Gillian had simply been careless about the gas fireplace and that she had forgotten to open the window. After all, what was I to suppose?"

"The next time," Jill went on quietly, "was when my car brakes failed to work when I was coming down Long Hill. I'd just had the car overhauled. But—it had been tampered with. What saved me was that big sand pit. I turned into it. All that happened then was a couple of cracked ribs."

Bennett nodded at Allen's skeptical glance. "Of course it happened just as she says. But she is a fast driver and—"

"But today—it's the third time." Jill's teeth began to chatter. "I-I'm—f-f-frightened."

Bennett took off his white linen jacket and put it over her shoulders.

"I'll drive you home. You have a chill. You'll get pneumonia if we aren't careful." For a moment his troubled expression reminded her of his son Chester. "And I thought we were taking such good care of you."

"Not good enough," Allen snapped. "I'll put in a call for Roger Clayton at once. We'll have to take immediate steps for Miss Bellamy's protection."

"Protection from what?" Bennett asked.

"I don't know," Allen admitted. "But there's one thing I do know. If anything happened to her we would be blamed. And, frankly, we can't afford it."

III

The law firm of Garrison, Harper & Jennings occupied a floor high in the tower of the Chrysler Building. From its windows one could see not only New York City spread out below, but the rivers on either side of Manhattan Island.

Even after a year with the firm Jim Trevor still felt himself drawn to the windows, was still intoxicated by the magnificence of the views in whatever direction he looked. Surely nowhere in the world could there be as exciting a city as this. Someday he was going to win a place for himself here, an honorable place.

Life had tapped gay, ambitious Jim Trevor on the shoulder when his father was stripped of his property, and it shook him wide awake to its realities. Until then, he had expected that the future, like the past, would be cushioned and pleasant. Luxuries were to be had by the mere signing of a check. His career, when he had decided on it, would be made easy because of his father's money, his father's position, and the wide circle of his father's influential friends.

Overnight, all that was wiped away. When the first shock was over, Jim had applied the refrigerating process of cold reason to the situation. He took stock of himself and his abilities and set to work to plan a new life. Now, after four years of concentrated effort, he had his foot on the first rung of the ladder.

Jim folded the letter which he had just received from his father and put it carefully away in an inside pocket. As usual, Andrew Trevor had written cheerfully, with interest in Jim's work and a heartening confidence that, before many years had passed, he would be a partner in this law firm whose reputation was second to none.

"Mr. Trevor?"

Jim turned away from the window. A trim young woman was smiling at him. A number of young women smiled at this tall young man with his finely cut features, good jaw and steady gray eyes. He returned the smile. He would have been taken aback if anyone told him how irresistibly charming his smile was.

"Yes, Miss Andrews?"

"Mr. Garrison would like to see you at once."

Jim followed her to the big corner office occupied by the senior partner of the firm, wondering why he had been sent for. He had never been in the office since the day when he had been hired. Had he blundered on the Wicks case? It was the first one he had handled alone. True, his methods of getting the information he needed may have been unorthodox. But he had won the case, and the proof of the pudding, as his old nurse used to say, was in the eating.

He squared his shoulders and went in to face the senior partner. The room was huge, deeply carpeted, with comfortable chairs, a desk whose shining surface contained only a blotter, a desk set and a framed photograph of the son Mr. Garrison had lost in Korea.

For a moment the sun blazing in nearly blinded Jim, then he went forward to face the man behind the desk. Garrison was a big man, white-haired, with a floridly handsome face and an impressive manner. Shrewd eyes studied the young man for a moment. Then he waved him to a chair beside his desk.

"Sit down, Trevor." He turned to his secretary. "I don't want to be disturbed until I call

30

you, Miss Andrews." He waited until she had closed the door quietly behind her. Then he turned to Jim, lighted a cigarette, and leaned back in the big leather chair.

"That was nice work you did on the Wicks case," he said casually.

Jim's face lighted in relief. "I'm glad you think so, sir." The disarming grin transformed him, made him seem more boyish. "Coming in here, I began to worry about it. I felt like a schoolboy being hauled up to the principal to take a shellacking."

Garrison was amused. "We like to put a man through his paces, see what he's capable of when he's left to his own devices. You came out all right."

For a moment he smoked in silence. Heavy draperies at the window left his own face in shadow while the revealing light fell on the face of the young lawyer. Plenty of intelligence there, Garrison thought in approval. Strength, too, but balanced by sensitivity and imagination. A bold courage in the way he had tackled the Wicks case.

Courage, too, in the way he had accepted the blow that fate had dealt him. No one had ever heard him complain about it. He had worked harder than anyone in his law class and he had tackled his job for the law firm

31

with energy, enthusiasm and a refreshing lack of arrogance. He was quick to give other people credit for their help and he displayed a healthy humility about his own lack of experience.

"I understand," Garrison said aloud, "you decided not to use the investigators we usually employ. You worked entirely on your own."

"I didn't know exactly what I was looking for," Jim admitted. "I just knew there must be something, so I went on digging by myself until I found it."

Garrison nodded. He pressed out his cigarette. He seemed to have all the time in the world.

"Trevor," he said at last, "we've got a curious situation here. It may be a mare's nest, it may be deadly serious.

"Deadly serious," he repeated. "Literally. One of our clients was a man named Thomas Bellamy. Wealthy man. Very wealthy. His hobby was art and he had enough money to devote his life to hunting down treasures. He built a fine collection, which he decided to bequeath to his home town.

"Three years ago, he died. He left a large sum of money to build a museum to house his collection and to add to it. The bulk of his estate he left to his daughter Gillian, who was then seventeen, and who is now our client."

Garrison looked at Jim, who nodded his comprehension.

"Bellamy appointed three governors to administer the art museum — Institute, he called it — and to look after his daughter until she is twenty-one. One of them was appointed her guardian and she lives at his house."

Garrison lighted another cigarette. "Bellamy made his daughter his heiress," he repeated, "but if she should die before she is twenty-one, her money is to go to the Institute, where, with fairly loose provisions for the maintenance of the building and the collection, it is practically at the disposal of these three governors."

Jim nodded again, wondering what this all had to do with him. "That is a very dangerous situation," he commented.

"Very. It's the only foolish thing I ever knew Bellamy to do. I tried my best to talk him out of it, to get him to permit me to rewrite his will so it would be airtight. But he wouldn't listen."

Jim grinned. "Sometimes I think people call in lawyers only to find out how they can do what they want to do; they never seem to want to know what they ought to do."

"How right you are! Well, one of the governors," Garrison said slowly, "got in touch with me at my home last night. He was considerably upset. It appears . . ." The lawyer crushed out his cigarette and leaned forward, his voice more incisive. Here it comes, Jim thought. "It appears that recently Gillian Bellamy claims to have had three serious accidents: gas turned on in the night in her bedroom; failing brakes on her car that resulted in a couple of cracked ribs; and an induced plunge into a river, in which she might easily have drowned."

Jim sat bolt upright. "Attempts at murder, sir?"

"I don't know," Garrison said heavily. "Perhaps coincidence, perhaps overheated imagination, perhaps—real trouble. Well, that's where you come in. I want you to find out just what is happening to Gillian Bellamy and whether she's in danger. If she is—you're to stop it."

A slow grin widened Jim's mouth. "This is an assignment I'm going to like."

Garrison, watching him, made no comment.

"What instructions do you want to give me?"

Garrison considered. "I've been thinking a

lot about this. I'm trusting you to see it through on your own initiative, as you did in the Wicks case; to prevent a tragedy, if that is what is at stake; and to see that nothing is done to discredit this law firm. In a sense, you can regard yourself as my ambassador."

Jim lifted his head. "I'll try not to disappoint you, sir."

"Good! Now, as long as we don't know what the situation is, I don't want you to go openly, under your own name. I'm sending you up as chauffeur to the trustee who called me. He's decided to go back there and take up residence for a while. He'll know who you are, of course. No one else. You'll be—let's see. Peter Carr. He tells me your duties won't be onerous, so you'll have plenty of leisure in which to scout around. Under cover, naturally."

Jim's smile was wry. "An ambassador in chains," he commented.

Garrison, it seemed to him, was watching his reactions rather oddly. "Any objection to that?"

"Of course not. As long as you feel it would be helpful. No other instructions?"

"Use your eyes and ears and your common sense. Find out what you can about those three governors, including the one who is ostensibly hiring you. Get a good look at Gillian Bellamy. Size her up for yourself. After all, you are nearer her age than her governors are. You'll understand better what she's really like. See whether she's the kind of girl who imagines she is being persecuted or whether she simply wants to dramatize herself. Look into the background of those men. Of course, we'll give you any assistance we can from here."

Jim nodded. "That seems clear enough. When do I go?"

"Tomorrow. There will be a chauffeur's uniform at your apartment tonight. Any more questions?"

This time Jim laughed outright. "Yes, sir. Where do I go?"

"Mapleville, Connecticut." The older man's eyes were sharp on Jim's face.

Jim pushed back his chair, leaped to his feet. "No!" he said explosively. "No! I'm sorry, sir, but I can't go there."

IV

Garrison asked quietly, "Why not?"

There was a long pause before Jim answered carefully. "I couldn't get away with being Peter Carr there. I—lived there once for a short time. There are people who know me."

"How many?"

"Not many," Jim said after a long pause. "It was just a few summer vacations while I was in college."

"Sit down, Trevor," Garrison said, and the younger man dropped into his chair. "This firm, as you know, has a fine reputation. Every year the law schools of the country recommend their most promising graduates to us, hoping they will have a chance to work with us."

"I know that, sir," Jim said huskily. "Don't think I haven't appreciated my luck in being chosen."

"We weigh the candidates carefully, their scholastic records, their general intelligence, their personalities, their characters. After we have selected a man we watch the way he operates. Sooner or later, we test him, as we tested you in the Wicks case, by leaving him on his own. There's a reason for that. We want to see how the man behaves when he has to make his own decisions and take full responsibility for his own mistakes. The law is man's wisest and best safeguard against savagery. It is civilization's barricade against man's jungle impulses. You agree?"

"Yes sir," Jim said fervently.

"We back our men with all we have, once we have admitted them, but we expect them to back us, too. If you are categorically refusing to accept this assignment—" He spread out his hands in a helpless gesture.

"You mean I'll be finished here," Jim said steadily.

Garrison made no answer. He waited patiently.

After a moment, Jim got up and went to stand at the window, staring with blind eyes down at the traffic so far below that the cars and trucks were beetles, the scurrying human beings were ants, moving when invisible lights changed, as though taking part in a fantastic dance.

There no longer seemed to be a limitless vista. The people down below moved as though on strings, helpless, people on a treadmill, people in a trap.

Jim came back to the desk, his face white, but his voice steady.

"I think, sir, I had better explain why I can't go to Mapleville."

"There's no rush. Take your time."

"My father left Mapleville four years ago, under a cloud," Jim said bluntly. "He moved up there when Mother died. Even on my brief visits home from school I could see that he had made himself the town benefactor. Everyone loved him. He is just about the most generous man I ever knew. A good man if there ever was one. But he is gullible, trusting." There was a bitter look on Jim's face. "At least, he was."

"Go on."

"Well, a guy came along with some sort of oil deal. I never knew the particulars and later I didn't like to ask. He was an old acquaintance of Dad's. Dad believed in him. He put about everything he had in that oil scheme. And even that wasn't enough. Being Dad, he wanted all his friends to share in this bonanza. Because they trusted him implicitly, they plunged."

Jim gave a mirthless laugh. "Dad lost his shirt, of course. But so did the people who trusted him. That would have been bad enough, God knows, but somehow a rumor got around that Dad had known all about the swindle. He had deliberately tricked his friends into plunging and he'd made a fortune out of them. No one believed he hadn't deliberately cleaned them out in order to line his own pockets. So at last he left—under a cloud. He was bewildered and heartsick.

"His health broke and he went out to the Southwest to recuperate. He cashed in his insurance and bought stock in an unknown oil field. And struck oil! As soon as he could, he wrote to Mapleville. He wanted to know how much money the people had lost so he could make full restitution. He got back a letter saying the town wanted nothing more to do with him."

Unexpectedly, Garrison smiled. "Then it looks to me, young man, as though you had two motives in going back to Mapleville: our job and your own—to clear your father's name."

"How can you make people believe what they don't want to believe, sir?"

"That's up to you, isn't it, Trevor? Up to

you and your unorthodox methods." Garrison waited a moment. "Is that your only objection to taking on this job for us?"

Jim's hands clenched on the arms of his chair.

"Oh, there's something else, is there?" Garrison said shrewdly. "Is it a girl?"

Jim nodded without speaking.

"And she turned you down, of course, after your father's—after your father left town."

Jim made no reply. His lips tightened.

"Well, Trevor, are you going to let personal considerations stand in the way?"

Jim took a long breath. "No sir. But if she—she's still there, she will recognize me."

"We'll take a chance on it," Garrison decided. "You're to report tomorrow morning at ten o'clock at the Plaza. Ask for Mr. Roger Clayton."

Jim gave a muffled exclamation.

"He will tell you where to pick up his car. Then you are to drive him and his daughter to Mapleville. You'll have quarters over his garage. He lives next door to William Bennett, another of the governors, Gillian Bellamy's guardian, so you'll have a chance to see something of her. All clear?"

"Yes, sir. I'll pick up Mr. Clayton at ten

tomorrow at the Plaza. Mr. Clayton—and Denise."

That night, while Jim packed his bags and arranged to close his apartment for an indefinite length of time, his thoughts were in a turmoil. He was going back to Mapleville, though he had sworn never to set foot in the place again. He was going to see Denise Clayton once more. And see her, he reminded himself grimly, as her father's chauffeur.

He couldn't do it. No one could expect that much of a man. He couldn't. To reappear in her life not, as he had dreamed countless times, successful, his father's name cleared, with a fortune he had earned himself to offer her, but as Roger Clayton's employee. No, he couldn't do it.

He started toward the telephone. He'd tell Mr. Garrison the deal was off. And then? Then the doors of Garrison, Harper & Jennings would be closed to him. Forever. The finest opportunity he could ever have would be lost.

Jim paced the floor, hands clenching and unclenching. His father would say nothing. Not a single word of condemnation, not a breath of criticism. But he would be disappointed and he had had so much disappointment.

Jim thought of his father, big and bluff, laughing and gay. He remembered how the gaiety had gradually disappeared, killed by the distrust of his friends that had cut so deep. They had all turned against him. If his son were to fail him, too, there would be little left.

Garrison had not appeared to be unduly upset by Jim's account of his father's catastrophe and disgrace. He had suggested that this might be an opportunity to clear his father's name. Jim took a long breath, squared his shoulders. All right. He would do it. Though it meant destroying his dreams forever.

Before he could change his mind, he sat down to write to his father. He told him of the assignment Garrison had given him and of what he hoped to accomplish on his double mission. He went out to mail the letter at once.

"And remember," he had concluded. "that any letter to me in Mapleville must be addressed to Peter Carr."

When he came back to the apartment his heart was lighter. No turning back now.

The telephone was ringing.

"Trevor? This is Roger Clayton speaking."

"Yes, Mr. Clayton."

Jim had met Clayton only once during his whirlwind courtship of Denise, but the sound of the big confident voice brought a clear picture of the man. A heavy-set man with iron-gray hair, blunt features and driving energy. A man who bore all the outward signs of success.

"I've just been talking to Garrison. We seem to be all set. Did you find the uniform? . . . Right size? . . . Good. My car's at the Coliseum Garage, a Cadillac. I'm sending a messenger over to you now with the ticket. Pick us up here at the Plaza in the morning. Ten sharp."

"Yes, sir." Jim's voice was colorless.

"I've decided to open my house and spend the rest of the summer in Mapleville. As I understand it, your real job is to find out if there's any truth in this weird story about the Bellamy girl. It's a small town and people talk. Unless you've got anything to report to me we'll keep our relations strictly employer and employee. That clear?"

"Yes, sir." Jim's hand whitened as he increased his tight hold on the telephone.

"Oh, by the way, I had to explain to my daughter. Not about your job up there. No woman can keep a secret. But that I was

44

hiring you as my chauffeur for a while and you would take the name of Peter Carr. She suggests we call you Peters. More in character, she thought. All right with you?''

Jim's voice could not force its way through his closed throat. He cleared it. "All right, sir."

"Then, good night, Peters."

Jim set down the telephone. Peters! He could hear Denise make the suggestion, laughing. Denise, the golden girl whom he had loved, whom he still loved. He couldn't help it. She was the prettiest thing he had ever seen. Her hair, like Portia's — *her sunny locks, like golden fleece*. Denise made him think of poetry always. That had amused her, too.

For two summers he had pursued her, crazy about her, hanging on her words, watching her soft blue eyes, her red lips, listening to her voice, enraptured by everything she said. If ever a boy had been infatuated, he had been the one. And in the four years since she had sent him away, he had never got over it.

They had been sitting on the edge of the Clayton swimming pool when Jim had begged her to marry him.

"You are asking me to marry you?" Denise

45

had said incredulously.

"I know it's a lot to ask." How humble he had sounded, Jim thought now, looking back. "You could have anyone you wanted."

Denise had laughed. "How many more years will you be in school?"

"I'd planned on law school but I can give that up and get a job right now."

"A job doing what? For how much?" She had stood up then and he had scrambled to his feet, a tall gangling boy, too thin, shaking with the intensity of his feelings.

"You know what?" she demanded unexpectedly. "You can't support a wife and you know it. You haven't a penny to your name. Do you know what you are, Jim Trevor? You're a fortune hunter. Now get out of my life!"

V

The news item was at the foot of a column of print, the headline so small that Jill nearly passed over it entirely. If she hadn't been reading the newspaper almost word for word, she would not have seen it at all.

The paper was a shield between her and the Bennetts and she was reluctant to put it down, to face the reproachful eyes of her hosts.

It had been Friday when she had taken her unexpected plunge in the river. All day Saturday, at the insistence of Mrs. Bennett, she had stayed in bed, though she felt no ill effects from her accident. She hadn't even caught cold. But bed had been a refuge as the paper was now. For Maud Bennett, with a mother's awareness of her son's disappointment, knew that she had refused to marry Chester. Neither of the Bennetts had

47

mentioned it, of course, but their knowledge was clear in Mr. Bennett's reproachful eyes, in his wife's new restraint. She was doing all she could to show no difference in her attitude, but she felt her son's pain and she could not forgive Jill for having caused it.

Chester had been solicitous and kind when his father had brought her back to the house, soaking wet and chilled, but he made no attempt to force his attentions on her. After his first shocked exclamation he had insisted on knowing what had happened. He had listened intently, his face white with strain.

"But Jill, my dear, no one would deliberately have thrown rocks at you."

"That's what I told her," his father declared. "Take my word, some kids were fooling around and got scared when they realized what they had done."

"But the railing had been ripped away," Jill said stubbornly. "Someone planned it that way."

Mrs. Bennett had intervened then to take Jill to her room and get her out of her soaking clothes. She had seemed to be more distressed over the ruin of the new dress than over the fact that Jill might have been drowned.

Mrs. Bennett, Jill had come to realize, was

48

a woman to whom only her own imaginary ailments were real. When she encountered an actual problem she was able to dismiss it as though it didn't exist. A ruined dress she could worry about happily. But a deliberate attempt to injure her husband's ward was something to which she could turn deaf ears. Unpleasant things didn't happen to anyone but herself.

This morning, Chester had gone across the lawn to greet Roger Clayton's daughter, who had appeared at the swimming pool. Jill could hear them laughing together.

She looked up over the paper and saw the girl, in a pale green bathing suit, golden hair bright in the sunlight. She heard the girl laugh and caught Mrs. Bennett's eyes. A faint smile played around the older woman's mouth and Jill thought, She hopes I'll be jealous. But she's mistaken. I wish with all my heart that Chester would fall in love with another girl.

She plunged back into the paper and saw the news item:

MASTERPIECE ACQUIRED BY NEW OWNER
The head of a Greek god, known as The Man with the Broken Nose, said to be the work of Praxiteles, has been added to the

sculpture collection of Hendrick Freelton of Cincinnati, Ohio, and will be on display, by card only, during the week of August 10.

The Man with the Broken Nose. Jill put down the paper, too preoccupied to worry about the Bennetts' scrutiny. There couldn't possibly be two such heads by Praxiteles, both damaged in the same way, and the original belonged to her father. It had been one of his favorite possessions, one of the few pieces he kept with him. She remembered seeing it over the mantel in the apartment in Paris, in a niche in that cold palace in Florence where they had rented two floors for a year, on a pedestal in the library of their country house in England.

The telephone rang and Mr. Bennett heaved himself out of his chair and went inside. Jill closed her eyes, trying to recall the position of the head in the Institute. Curious, she had never noticed before that it was not on display. Her guardian came back.

"That was Clayton," he said. "Suggested I drop in for a chat. I won't be gone long. An hour at the outside. I suppose, Maud, you'd better ask him and his daughter to dinner.

They'll want to meet Gillian. And they have a house guest, a cousin, a man named Holt. Dan Holt."

"I'll write a note now and you can take it over with you. Will Tuesday be all right?" She followed her husband into the house.

On impulse, Jill got up. She had caused so much disturbance by speaking of her accident that she wanted to be sure her suspicions were justified before she said anything now about the Praxiteles bust. Mr. Clayton had changed his plans and come here because of her. Mr. Allen had, quite frankly, not believed her. She hadn't understood his attitude until her guardian explained. Abraham Allen wanted to be State Senator, and any hint of scandal in the management of the Institute would be a disaster for him.

"Abe is the cranky type," Bennett had told Jill with a chuckle. "I wouldn't put it past him to think you are doing this on purpose."

"Well, if he thinks I jumped into the river just to make things tough for him," Jill sputtered, "Why, it's too ridiculous."

"You have to make allowances, my dear," Bennett said. "Abe is anxious not to have anything affect his popularity."

"Popularity!" Jill's gale of laughter had swept her guardian along with it like a high

51

wind and he chuckled. "But it's not funny to him, poor devil!" he said soberly.

So this time Jill preferred to check for herself before she mentioned The Man with the Broken Nose to the governors. If the bust were tucked away somewhere in the Institute she would feel silly. And yet it was beyond the range of probability that there could be two heads by the same sculptor, both with the nose broken off.

She sauntered away from the house, glad to escape for a while from the Bennetts. If only Chester would take an interest in that very pretty girl next door. It was awkward to have to live in his house, knowing how disappointed he was, how aggrieved his mother felt. For the first time Jill looked forward to her twenty-first birthday and freedom. Nine more months.

Yet the thought of the money she would have oppressed her. It would be a great responsibility. Of course, the governors would probably continue to handle it for her. That had been her father's idea. Unless, of course, she married a man who was competent to administer her estate.

She remembered the letter her father had left for her. She had read it so often that she knew it by heart.

You will marry, of course. Some lucky man will find in you a loyal and loving wife, ready to face problems with courage, to create a real partnership, to bring laughter and sunlight into his home. Like that line I have quoted so often: "You came and the sun came after."

Whether he is rich or poor does not matter. Follow your heart. You have an understanding heart that rarely misleads you. But the money I leave you is a trust. If your husband is to handle it, he must be a man of unimpeachable honesty, a man whose word needs no bond, a man whose sense of responsibility is stronger than his personal ambition.

Such a man you richly deserve. Such a man I hope you will find and marry.

Jill made her way cautiously over the footbridge to the Institute, edging past the broken place in the railing, which had not yet been repaired. Few people came this way in a motor age; the chief crossing for the Institute was by way of a motor bridge two blocks away. She hurried as much as she dared, half expecting the sound of rocks striking near her on the bridge. She felt herself cringing. Her ankle under its sheer stocking still showed a raised, discolored lump.

There were only a few people in the Institute, peering at glass cases of jewelry and watches and fans, studying paintings, looking at statues. Jill went swiftly from room to room, making a quick but meticulous survey of every object. The Man with the Broken Nose was not there.

The only person on duty was the guard, Joe, who beamed at her from a doorway where he could keep an eye on the exhibits.

"All right, little lady?" he asked.

"Except for this." Jill showed him her ankle.

The old man's face hardened. "I'd like to get my hands on the one who did that," he said fiercely.

"Joe, do you remember a bust, a man's head with the nose chipped off? I can't seem to find it, and you know every piece in this place."

"Sure I remember it," Joe said promptly. "Your Daddy set a lot of store by that head. Never could figure it myself, when the nose had been broken off. What's the use of keeping busted statuary? Don't make sense to me when you can afford the best like your Daddy could. But he said it was—how many

54

hundred years old?—and beautiful work-
manship. When I was driving for him in
England—everyone going the wrong way,
remember?—he had it sitting up on a pedestal like."

"But where is it now?" Jill demanded. "I've
looked everywhere and I can't find it."

Joe scratched his head. "Now, then," he
began slowly, "that's a funny thing." He
broke off to say, "Hey, there, kids, don't lean
on that glass case." He turned back to Jill.
"Real funny, if you ask me. I don't remember
seeing it here at all."

"Not ever?"

Joe stood in thought for a moment, then
shook his head decisively. "Not ever."

Knowing the guard's photographic memory, Jill was sure that the bust had never been
in the Institute.

She left quickly, but when she was out of
doors she slowed down, her winged eyebrows
drawn together in a frown. What could have
happened to the Praxiteles bust? Had the
man from Cincinnati really bought it? But
how was that possible? She sighed to herself.
She would simply have to bring up the
mystery of the missing head before the governors. She dreaded Mr. Allen's sharp
tongue, his skeptical attitude.

Not wanting to return to the Bennett house just yet, Jill sat down in the shade of a big maple tree, her hands clasped around her knees, and looked down at the sleepy river. There was one way she could check on the bust, find out whether it had ever been among the items destined for the Institute. Her father had had a complete catalogue made of his collection and it had been carefully checked, item by item, when the collection was installed in the Institute. Tomorrow, she would ask her guardian for the catalogue and examine it before she caused any more disturbance among the governors. There was always the possibility, remote as it seemed, that her father had arranged for the sale before his death.

Having made up her mind as to her course of action, Jill dismissed it from her thoughts. Her eyes traveled over the dingy warehouse across the river. What an eyesore! That was something else she would have to discuss with the governors. There must be fifteen acres or more of land turning to weeds. A magnificent spot for a garden and lawns. And maybe peacocks, she thought dreamily. Maybe a pool with flamingos. Maybe —

She looked up. Something had caught her attention. She must be mistaken, she

56

decided. There was nobody in sight, nothing stirring in that deserted building.

She stared hard at the shabby warehouse. Something had moved! She was sure of it. Slowly her eyes traveled along the dilapidated building, along the rows of windows on which the sun was shining. That was queer. Most of the windows were filthy but the glass in those on the upper right side sparkled. Now why?

She got slowly to her feet. One of them seemed to be broken. Broken? No, it was wide open. As she looked at it, something white moved in that open space and the window was pulled down.

Jill went quickly across the footbridge, too preoccupied this time to worry about the broken railing or the fear of a new bombardment of rocks. Across the river she picked her way through the weeds until she noticed that a path had been beaten through them to the door. A door with paint peeling off. A door — she looked more closely — with a shining new lock. A door that swung open silently on oiled hinges as her hand pressed against it.

For a moment Jill stood quietly, waiting for her eyes to adjust to the dark interior after the brilliant light of the morning sun. Then she looked around her. The warehouse seemed vast, a dingy barnlike building, empty of people or of objects.

The door of what must have been a small enclosed office stood open. Jill peered inside, saw boxes and crates stacked on the floor, each marked with an odd symbol: Φ.

VI

If it hadn't been for the footsteps she would have left the building at once. There was nothing furtive about them. Someone was walking around the upper floor without any attempt at concealment.

She called up the ramshackle stairs, "Hey, up there!"

"Who's that?" shouted a startled voice.

"What are you doing in this building?"

Someone was running down the stairs now. Looking up, Jill saw first a man's shoes on the treads, then dark trousers. He turned at the landing and she could see him — a tall man with stormy eyes. They looked at each other in mutual surprise.

"You again!" he said in a tone of disgust. "What are you doing here?"

"That's the explanation I want from you," Jill said crisply.

He leaned against the post at the foot of the stairs, one hand in his pocket, looking at her with leisurely impertinence. Once more Jill was conscious of those X-ray eyes with their ill-tempered eyebrows.

"Well, now," he said lazily, "can you think of any good reason why I should owe you any explanation? Let me give you a tip, sister. Don't interfere in what doesn't concern you."

"This does concern me," Jill retorted. "The building belongs to me and you have no right to be in it without permission."

He arched his eyebrows. "Quite a little autocrat, aren't you? Must be nice to think you own the earth." There was open mockery in his tone.

"But I don't—" Jill began, in hot protest.

He detached himself from the post and took a step forward. Jill overcame an instinctive desire to back away, to leave him in control of the situation. She forced herself not to retreat, though her heart was beating hard and fast.

"Suppose you run along, like a good little girl," he drawled. "And don't try to tell me what to do. Military dictators are bad enough, but female dictators—the Lord preserve us! Get going now. I don't want you in my hair again. Is that clear? Scram!"

Jill's jaw dropped, she stared at him, color ebbing. "Who are you? Wh-why did you throw those rocks at me? Why did you try to drown me?"

His expression was as blank as her own. Then his eyes moved suddenly, looking away from her face, over her shoulder. Jill felt rather than heard the movement behind her. Then something struck her between the shoulders and she pitched forward on her face into the little office and the door slammed behind her. She heard a key turn in the lock.

For a moment she was dazed. The breath had been knocked out of her, her head had struck against a wooden crate. Then she could breathe again and she tried to sit up, was caught in a spinning universe and waited helplessly for the dizziness to subside, for the sickness to ebb, for her sight to clear.

Outside the door she heard the big man's voice raised in a shout. "You fool! What do you think you're doing?"

There was a subdued murmur.

"That's your problem," the big man snapped. "But I didn't bargain for knocking women around."

But you don't mind scaring them half to death, Jill thought.

Another mumble. Jill strained her ears but she caught no more words. The two men seemed to be going away.

At last she pulled herself cautiously to her feet. She listened, holding her breath. Nothing moved. She had a curious conviction that she was alone in the building. She tried the door but it was locked.

There was a rustling near her; something moved. A rat.

The girl looked desperately around. On top of one of the boxes was a hammer. She picked it up. At least, she thought, her heart leaping and racing, she had something with which to defend herself. A rat scuttled across her ankle and she screamed. In a frenzy she pounded on the door with the hammer.

"Let me out! Let me out!"

Someone was running. The big surly man again? Probably. She was afraid of him, but anything was better than the rat.

The handle of the door was turned. There were two rats now. Jill's scream rose wildly in the air. "Help! Hurry!"

"Okay," a man called. "Hold everything. Keep back. Stand away from the door. I'm going to try to break it down."

She heard the footsteps—moving away? Surely he wouldn't leave her here. Then they were coming back at a run. There was a splintering crash, the door burst open, and a man catapulted into the room, his weight flinging her back against a pile of boxes.

He caught her in his arms, pulled her to her feet, and looked into her face. She stood in the circle of his arms, staring into level gray eyes. She knew him, she thought in that first moment of surprised recognition. She knew him well. Then she realized that he was a stranger whom she had never seen before.

He released her gently, keeping one hand on her arm.

"All right now?"

"Yes, but let's get out of here. There are rats." Her voice shook uncontrollably and yet she was no longer afraid.

He growled deep in his throat like a dog about to charge. "Who locked you in here?"

She shook her head. "I don't know. He was behind me. He—pushed. They've both gone."

"Both? Here, let's get out in the sunlight before we talk." He led her outside, found a clear spot on the ground where she sat down.

Her head hurt when she moved and it made her dizzy to raise her eyes. She sat quickly, waiting for her heart to slow down, for the world to grow steady, for the dizziness to pass so that she could look up without a sense of whirling blindly into space.

For a moment he waited in silence. When at last she looked up at him she saw a tall young man, with square shoulders and a deceptively slender body, because he had great strength. He was one of the best-looking men she had ever seen but he did not appear to be aware of his good looks nor to be desirous of capitalizing on them, as most handsome men did. He had a strong jaw, a fine and sensitive mouth, and gray eyes that looked searchingly into her own.

This is ridiculous, she told herself in a panic. You're imagining things. No one falls in love at first sight. It isn't true. Except — Juliet.

"Juliet," she heard herself say aloud and felt color flooding her cheeks. She was appalled but helpless before her own self-betrayal.

There was a quick flare in his eyes, almost as though he had understood her meaning, but that was impossible, of course.

"Will you be all right here?" he asked. He had a quiet voice.

She nodded. Then she asked in alarm, "Where are you going?"

"I just want to look around."

"You—please be careful."

He smiled at her, a smile that transformed his face and warmed her cold heart that had been so chilled by fear.

"I'll be very careful. I have reason to be—now. And don't move. Wait for me."

She nodded again. After a long look he turned away, went into the warehouse. It was nearly twenty minutes before he came back to her, time that passed as though it had never been, while Jill excoriated herself for acting like a lovesick schoolgirl. By the time he reached her side she was able to look at him with cool detachment.

"Did you find—anyone?"

He shook his head. "No one there," he said, "but someone has been using the place for something. Upstairs I found a padlocked door. I couldn't break it down." He grinned. "Probably that's just as well. I already have to account to the owner for breaking and entering."

"You needn't worry about that. I'm the owner. Oh, I am Gillian Bellamy."

"You!" There was a long silence before he said, "I am—Peter Carr. I'd better take you home. You don't look to me as though you were up to much walking. That's a nasty lump you've got on your head. Is your car here?"

She shook her head. "I'm still afraid to drive it. Anyway, I don't want to go home. Not yet. Oh, I know what. Take me to Aunt Sally."

He stood unmoving for a moment. Then he leaned down, took her hand, and drew her smoothly to her feet. As they walked away from the warehouse, he said in his slow quiet voice, "Perhaps you'd better tell me what happened."

She found herself pouring out the story, beginning with the impression that something was moving in the building and seeing an upstairs window being shut, and ending with the man behind her who had given her a shove.

"You're sure there were two of them?" he asked.

She nodded emphatically and then clutched her head. "Ouch!"

"And the one behind you was a man?"

"Why—" her eyes widened—"I supposed so. The one I saw—he nearly knocked me down the other day. I think he's the one who threw the rocks at me."

"What!"

Jill told him about the rocks, the plunge in the river, and Abraham Allen's flat disbelief in her account of the accident. Once she had started to talk, the floodgates opened.

This man was incredibly easy to talk to. It seemed as though she had been talking to him all her life. She told him about the gas fireplace in her bedroom that had been turned on in the night and the window that had been shut. She told him about the car brakes that had failed.

His hand tightened spasmodically on her arm and she looked up to see how his jaw muscles rippled. Then his hand relaxed.

"How many people know about these—accidents?"

"The Bennetts and the governors at the Institute. That's all. Except," she added, "whoever is doing this to me."

"Any other—queer happenings?"

"Well, The Man with the Broken Nose," she said, "is missing."

He laughed. "Missing—one man with a broken nose. Do you want to find him?"

"Not a man. Just a head," she explained.

"Good heavens! Do you mean to tell me there's a head walking around without a body attached to it?"

Jill's soft gurgle of laughter brought an answering smile to his eyes before it reached his lips. She told him about the mystery of the Praxiteles bust which her father had loved and which he seemed to have sold.

"And that's all that has happened?"

"All! With a lump on my head and one on my ankle and a memory of two cracked ribs and — and — well, I think it's enough, don't you?"

"More than enough. It has stopped as of now," he told her without any particular emphasis. "It's over." He fumbled in his pocket and drew out a pipe with a curiously carved stem. "Do you mind if I smoke? It helps me think."

"Of course not."

They were in front of Mrs. Meam's house. Peter Carr knocked on the door. Mrs. Meam opened it at once, looked in surprise from Jill, her face and dress streaked with dirt, to the young man in slacks and white shirt.

"Gillian! What's happened, child?"

"Aunt Sally!" The girl flung herself into the arms of the older woman and burst into tears. Mrs. Meam rocked her gently, whispering soothing words.

When the paroxysm was over, Jill drew herself away, wiped her eyes and blew her nose. "Sorry," she said, her voice muffled. "Mrs. Meam, this is Peter Carr, who — who just got me out of an awful mess."

Mrs. Meam looked steadily at the young man. "Come in, both of you. I was just getting lunch. You'll stay, of course."

"Lunch!" Jill exclaimed. "Oh dear, I have a date for lunch and I'll have to go home to change. What time is it?"

Peter Carr took an old-fashioned hunting-case watch out of his pocket and opened it. Jill looked at it. Twelve-fifteen. She saw the initials inside the case: J.T.

In the parlor she poured out her story once more. Mrs. Meam listened intently. Now and then she turned to give a long scrutinizing look at the quiet young man. Not a hostile look, Jill thought, but a puzzled one.

"Well," she said when Jill had finished, "I don't like the sound of this at all. But I can tell you one thing. I'll bet I know who is behind this."

"What!" Peter and Jill spoke simultaneously.

Mrs. Meam nodded, her pleasant face grim. "That man you described with the queer eyes that see right through you. That's my lodger, John Jones."

VII

"Now if you get the least bit tired, Gillian, you just excuse yourself and go straight up to bed."

In a bottle-green crepe dress, Maud Bennett looked sallow and old. Even when she tried to speak cheerfully her voice had a querulous, plaintive tone. And yet, Jill thought, with a devoted husband and loving son, a more than comfortable life and good health, she had small reason to be plaintive.

They were standing beside the long dining table, checking the flowers. Mrs. Bennett made a sharp survey of polished damask, of silver and crystal. Although she had an adequate and well-trained staff, she always complained of exhaustion and nervous headache by the time she had prepared for a dinner party.

How little joy she got out of living, the girl

70

thought, watching the older woman's petulant frown. Her greatest satisfaction seemed to come with the description of her ailments. Obscure ailments, for the most part. So obscure that the doctors never believed that she really suffered.

"Tired!" Jill laughed to conceal her irritation. "Tired by a small dinner party?"

For days the Bennetts had been treating her as though she were an invalid. She ought to see a doctor, Mrs. Bennett declared. She ought to go away for a while, have a complete change, Chester said. She was accident-prone, Mr. Bennett said. That was a sure sign of nervous tension somewhere. If she wasn't careful she'd even have a breakdown.

At the sound of the girl's laughter Mrs. Bennett turned to scrutinize her closely. In smoke-gray chiffon that swirled around her feet, her auburn hair burnished and softly waving, an emerald bracelet her father had given her clasped around one slim wrist, she was extraordinarily lovely. Though her manners were simple and charming, there was something regal about her poise, about the proud carriage of her head.

Mrs. Bennett felt a small stab of pain. If only Gillian would marry Chester. Surely she would come to it in time. He was a fine young man. If the girl had any sense she would realize just how fine he was. Her lips, around which lines had begun to form a network, tightened. Chester wasn't enterprising enough. He'd never push his just claims. Well, at least he had a mother who had his best interests at heart. There were ways and ways.

The doorbell rang and a maid came out of the kitchen, gave a swift look and went to open the door. Mrs. Bennett and Jill went into the living room to await their guests. Bennett and Chester were already there. The older man, as usual, looked like a penguin in dinner clothes, his face ruddy and cheerful. He was a perfect host. He loved entertaining and he enjoyed seeing his guests have a good time.

The guests entered the room, almost together. Abraham Allen shook hands with Mrs. Bennett and gave Jill a hand like a wet fish. Roger Clayton was accompanied by his daughter, and the cousin from New York, Dan Holt.

At first, Jill was conscious only of Roger Clayton. The man's prodigious vitality was like an electric charge in the air. He gave Jill a long searching look as they shook hands.

"I'm so glad to know you at last," Jill said warmly.

He met the direct look of her big eyes, saw the strength and tenderness of her smiling mouth, her proud carriage and gracious manner.

"The governors," he declared in his booming voice, "have certain enviable privileges." He kissed her cheek. "This is my daughter, Denise."

A golden girl, Jill thought, hair and skin and dress, with large blue eyes and a small red mouth.

"So you are the cause of all this trouble," Denise said and laughed gaily while her eyes summed up the Dior dress, the bracelet, the soft heavy masses of auburn hair.

I feel as though I had price tags all over me, Jill thought furiously. The Bellamy heiress. That's the way she wants to make me feel. But why?

"And Denise's cousin, Dan Holt," Roger Clayton said.

Dan Holt was slight and blond, with an amused expression when he looked at Denise and one of delighted surprise when he looked at Jill. His dinner clothes were obviously English tailored.

"You must be used to causing trouble," he

73

said, smiling at Jill. His hand closed over hers. "Heart-burning and jealousy. But when it comes to trouble, I'm your man."

Jill laughed as she freed her hand, and Denise's eyes narrowed while she observed the expression of interest on her cousin's face.

"I'm beginning to feel like Typhoid Mary," Jill confessed. "Wherever I go something seems to happen."

"But it does make you interesting, doesn't it, dear," Denise drawled.

Jill's face burned as though she had been slapped. It was Chester who stepped hastily into the breach and drew Denise away.

Dan Holt's look of amusement deepened. He winked at Jill. "When I think," he said sadly, "that I could have come up to Mapleville months ago —"

Mrs. Bennett had been watching them. She frowned. "I hope we'll see lots of you, Mr. Holt," she said, trying to infuse warmth in her manner. "I like having young people around. But Chester and Gillian — I think of them both as my children, of course — are like Siamese twins, always together. It's getting so I hardly ever see them apart."

Jill looked swiftly at the older woman, who turned away to talk to Roger Clayton. Mrs. Bennett was implying that she and Chester were engaged. For a moment she was tempted to deny it, but such a public statement would embarrass the woman, who had shown her much kindness, and it would hurt Chester, who had done nothing to deserve it. It would be better to tell Mrs. Bennett privately that she was not going to marry her son.

At dinner she found herself between Roger Clayton and Dan Holt. As soon as Mrs. Bennett had turned to Allen, who was on her left, Clayton was free to devote his attentions to Jill.

While she dipped shrimp in cocktail sauce and then sipped vichyssoise, he summed her up. This girl was too straightforward for self-dramatization, he decided. That eliminated one of the possibilities. There were three others. The accidents, four of them now, were a real attempt to injure her (Peter Carr's opinion). They were sheer coincidence, if they had ever happened at all (Allen's idea). She was accident-prone, unconsciously responsible for her own accidents because of overstrained nerves (Bennett's solution).

They had discussed it at length the day before. The things had really happened, Bennett said, his face drawn with worry. They must be stopped. The only way to protect

Gillian was to put her in a sanitarium where she could be watched.

"Watched?" Clayton had asked alertly.

"Well —" Bennett had hesitated, drumming his plump fingers on the table — "Gillian is a dear girl, a sweet child, but sometimes I'm afraid she is — over-imaginative, like her poor mother. You know about her mother, of course."

Clayton shook his head.

"No wonder. Bellamy never spoke of it. Poor soul. Poor woman. I just hope —" He let the subject drop.

"Miss Bellamy," Clayton said now, lowering his big voice so that he would not be overheard, "tell me about this last — adventure of yours. I couldn't get it quite clear from your guardian's account. What took you to a deserted warehouse in the first place?"

Jill explained that she had had an idea of demolishing the building and having the whole section landscaped and transformed into public gardens. Her eyes shone as she developed her plan.

"It could be made so beautiful," she concluded. "And people might get ideas for improving their own gardens." She broke off to laugh at her own excitement.

Whatever her mother may have been, there's nothing unhealthy in that mind, Clayton decided. It's sweet and sound and sane all the way through. Then, if we can dismiss four accidents as too much coincidence to swallow, and I think we must, that means someone is deliberately trying to hurt this lovely child.

No trace of his disturbance appeared in his manner. "But to get back to the warehouse—"

Jill sobered as she told him about seeing the open window and the white thing that had moved behind it. She had gone to investigate.

"Why?" Clayton asked.

Jill looked at him in surprise. "But I own the building. I'm responsible."

"I see," he said quietly. "But another time I'd leave it for someone who is better equipped to handle trouble."

"Next time," Jill said fervently, "I certainly will." She shivered.

With the serving of the main course, Mrs. Bennett called Clayton's attention back to herself and Dan Holt claimed Jill eagerly.

"All this time I've been waiting. Neglected. Ignored. Ill-treated."

Jill had a dazzling smile. "Poor man!"

"You see," he told her, "I can't afford to

waste so much time. All of twenty minutes. Think of the empty wasted years before I found you."

Jill was amused by his gay nonsense. She shook her head in commiseration. "I can't. It's too horrible."

"I'm glad you understand. But we'll make up for lost time. We'll—let's see—we have a tremendous number of things to do: dancing, swimming, tennis—oh, by the way, I'd better point out that, for this program, I'll need *all* your time."

"Your diffidence, Mr. Holt, is your most disarming quality."

The amused look was back on his face. "I have many delightful qualities. You'll see."

"I can hardly wait."

With the flaming dessert, Clayton neatly took Jill away from Holt again. "I want to hear more about that adventure of yours in the warehouse."

Jill told him about the new lock that had been put on the door. For some reason the door had not been closed. She had gone in, heard footsteps. The man had come down the stairs and had been very rude. Practically ordered her to go away and stay away. Then someone had pushed her into the little office and locked the door.

78

"There were rats," Jill said, her voice rising suddenly, "and I screamed."

She had caught the attention of the whole table. They were all listening.

"And then a man broke open the door and let me out."

"Where did he come from?" Chester asked sharply.

"Why—I don't know." Jill was startled. "He was just—passing, I suppose, and he heard me scream."

"He wasn't the man who locked you up in the first place?"

"Oh no!"

Clayton gave her an odd look. "What makes you so sure? Did you find out who he was?"

"His name was Peter Carr."

Something flickered behind Clayton's eyes. Denise leaned forward. "Why—" she began.

Her father stopped her with an abrupt gesture. "What did he do then?"

"He looked through the building, but there was a big padlock on a door upstairs and he couldn't search the place. So he took me to Aunt Sally's."

"I wasn't aware," Clayton said in surprise, "that you had any living relatives."

"She isn't really my aunt. Mrs. Sally

Meam. She keeps lodgers and she nursed me twice, once after the gas and again when I had broken ribs. And I've seen a lot of her since. She's been teaching me to cook."

"Cook!" Denise exclaimed in astonishment. "Why in the world—"

"I wanted to learn how," Jill said. Meeting the other girl's mocking eyes, she attempted no further explanation.

Dan Holt smiled. "They say it's the most direct way to a man's heart."

Denise laughed. "Heavens, she won't need that—not with all the Bellamy money. In fact, she won't need any other—attractions at all."

What she means, Jill thought, is that I haven't any attractions but the Bellamy money.

"Mrs. Meam," Allen said in his dry voice. "Oh, yes. She used to be Andrew Trevor's housekeeper, didn't she?"

"Trevor? Never heard of him," Bennett said.

"He was before your time," Clayton told him. "He left here—let's see, it must be at least four years ago."

"He had to leave," Allen said dryly.

"I suppose so." Clayton sounded regretful. "But I must admit that I liked the man tremendously. I never was as stunned as when I found out he was a crook. Everyone was stunned."

"I wasn't," Allen said. "It didn't surprise me. He was too smooth for me."

"And yet," Clayton pointed out. "Andy Trevor probably did more for Mapleville than any man who ever lived here."

Allen snorted.

"I know you've done a lot for the place, Abe," Clayton said hastily.

"But it's only since Trevor was driven out that anyone has noticed it," Allen snapped. "He had people thinking he was the great benefactor."

"Well, in a way he was," Clayton said, and after a look at him Allen made no further comment, though his nostrils were pinched and his mouth tightened.

"So this man Carr took you to Mrs. Meam," Clayton said, switching the conversation back to Jill.

"Yes, and she said she knew the man who was in the warehouse. Not the one who pushed me. I didn't see that one, of course, The other one. He's her lodger, John Jones."

"I think," Clayton said, "a little talk with Mr. Jones seems to be indicated."

"You know," Denise said, watching Jill

closely, "if I were you, Gillian, I'd wonder about this man Carr."

"Wonder what?" Jill asked, trying to keep her face serene, her voice level.

"Wonder if he was the man who pushed you, of course." The big blue eyes watched the color fade from Jill's face. Denise's red mouth smiled maliciously. "He must be quite a man." Then she observed her father's expression and she stopped as abruptly as though his hand had covered her mouth.

"I don't remember much about him," Jill said coolly. "Oh, there's another thing," she hastened on, eager to change the subject. "I almost forgot to tell you why I was near the warehouse at all."

She told him about the news item, which had stated that the Praxiteles bust had been sold to a collector in Ohio.

"I hunted all over the Institute but it isn't on display. By any chance, could it have been left out of my father's catalogue? And if it was listed, where is it now? It was one of my father's favorite pieces."

Bennett looked at her, his round face crimson. "Good heavens! That's impossible. There's some mistake. I'll check the catalogue in the morning and get in touch with the man in Ohio. Did you keep the newspaper clipping, Gillian?"

She nodded.

"And the warehouse," Allen said, his voice outraged. "That's part of our responsibility. What has it been used for, anyhow?"

"Just the storage of odds and ends," Bennett said. "I'll go through it with a fine-tooth comb and find out who has been using it."

"I'll help you, Dad," Chester offered.

"This is your vacation," his father reminded him. "I want you to enjoy every minute of it. Time enough for my problems later on."

"And now that's settled," Dan said to Jill, "let's get started on our own program. How about dinner and dancing at the inn on Thursday?"

"Oh, fun!" Denise said before Jill could answer. "We'll all go."

Dan gave his cousin an amused look. "Just what I had in mind," he assured her blandly.

VIII

"But I tell you," Jill protested, "I feel all right. I'm perfectly well. I haven't a single ache or pain."

"Just the same," Chester insisted doggedly, "I wish you'd go away. For a few weeks. Maine, perhaps, or that pretty place in New Hampshire with the wonderful views and the mountain climbing. Oh no, that wouldn't do. With your luck, you'd probably fall and break a leg. Or your neck."

"You're a gloomy gus." Jill laughed at him. Her eyes sparkled, her skin had a dewy glow. "Can't you see that I'm in perfect health?"

"But I want you to stay that way," Chester told her soberly. "What about going to New York? Think of all the big city has to offer: shops, theaters, museums—"

"New York in the summer?" Jill wailed. "And miss all this—trees in full bloom, the garden fairly singing with color, the air sweet as a gardenia. Oh, Chester!"

"Please go," he begged her. "I'm worried about you, Jill."

"But why?" Her smile faded as she saw his expression. "You think I'm in danger, don't you? Real danger."

"I don't know," he groaned. "I simply don't know. But we can't take any chances."

The telephone rang and she half rose from her chair. Then she heard the maid call Mrs. Bennett. She relaxed, her shoulders and the corners of her mouth drooping a little.

"Were you expecting a call?" Chester had not missed the eager expectation that had ended in disappointment.

"Nothing special," she said.

But it was special. Peter Carr had never telephoned. He hadn't said that he would, of course, but she had expected it. Every time the telephone rang her heart leaped. But it was always someone else who was calling.

"Who is it? Dan Holt?" Chester asked, his eyes still on her telltale face.

"Dan Holt?" She looked at him in surprise. "Oh, Dan Holt!"

He grinned. "I guess that takes care of Holt. Or else he thinks—" Chester broke off in discomfort.

Jill completed his sentence. "—that I am engaged to you. Chester, I meant to speak of it. Your mother—"

"She knows how I feel about you," Chester said awkwardly. "Mothers do, you know."

"No," Jill said, a lump in her throat that ached. "I don't know about mothers. I can't even remember mine."

"Poor kid. Well, I guess she just jumped to conclusions. She can't believe that anyone would be crazy enough to turn down her white-haired boy."

"But you must tell her," the girl said gently. "It's not fair—to any of us. And if people were to get the idea—you can see for yourself how embarrassing it might become, the awkward position we might all find ourselves in."

"I'll tell her," Chester said dully. He got up. "Well, I'll be off. Dad is going to make a careful check of your father's catalogue today, and then, if that Praxiteles bust is really missing, he'll get in touch with the Ohio collector. I'm going down to explore the warehouse and find out what has been going on there."

"But Chester, this is your vacation. Your father said that you weren't to bother."

"Yes, I know." Chester avoided her eyes.

"What are you going to do with yourself today?"

Jill was about to retort that what she did with her time did not concern Chester. Lately he had tried to find out in advance where she was going, what she was going to do, whom she expected to meet. But she couldn't snap at Chester, poor unhappy Chester.

"I'm going to the *Gazette* to see Mr. Loomis."

"Loomis? Oh, about that crazy scheme you were talking about last night? Stirring the local people—what was that highbrow phrase of yours?—'out of their civic lethargy'?"

"It's not a crazy scheme!" Jill retorted hotly.

"Well, I hope you know what you are doing," Chester said. "Until you are twenty-one, you can't do much without the approval of the governors and you are making Abe Allen absolutely furious."

"Why?" she asked in surprise.

"Because he has practically declared himself candidate for the Senate and he won't stand for having an outsider like you come along and stir people up."

"Oh," Jill said thoughtfully, "I hadn't thought of that."

"Don't get Allen against you, Jill. He could

be a bad enemy." Chester frowned.

"But I don't want to have any argument with him. All I want is to get people interested in what is going on, not to try to pit one candidate against another."

"Well, at least you can't say I haven't given you a fair warning. Then what are you going to do after you leave the *Gazette?*"

Jill swallowed her exasperation. "Aunt Sally is going to show me how to fix lobster."

Chester hesitated a moment as though reluctant to let her go. "Well, take care of yourself. I don't want anything more to happen to you."

"Neither do I," Jill said fervently. "But it won't."

She waved her hand and went quickly across the lawn, while Chester's eyes followed her. A slim girl with a graceful proud carriage, wearing a thin linen dress that matched her hair.

A voice hailed him. He turned to see Denise sitting on the edge of the swimming pool, golden hair shining in the sun.

Mockingly she sang the old song:

Won't you come over to my house?
Won't you come over and play?

He found himself smiling in sheer delight. How beautiful she was! The most bewitching girl he had ever seen.

"Well," he began dubiously, "I was going to—"

She stood up, pulled on her cap and ran to the diving board. "The water's perfect! You'll find bathing trunks in the men's bathhouse."

"Well—" For a moment he hesitated.

She made a perfect swan dive and came up at the far end of the pool. A white arm waved invitingly.

"Oh, well!" Chester ran across the lawn and closed the door of the small dressing room. One more day wouldn't make any difference, he told himself as he undressed hastily and got into bathing trunks. And Denise Clayton wasn't the kind of girl you turned down. Not if you expected her ever to notice you again.

He ran out to find her waiting at the edge of the pool. Her smile made him a hopeless victim, willing to become a carpet for her to walk on. She saw her power and took immediate advantage of it.

"How nice of Gillian to let you off the leash for a little while," she said sweetly. "I'll race you to the end of the pool." They dived in together.

The clicking of the type writer keys broke off as Jill entered the office of the Mapleville *Gazette*. The editor pushed back his green eyeshade.

"Be with you in a minute. I want to finish this story about the church supper. Turkey and fixings. Here—" He pushed typewritten yellow pages across the table. "My editorial. You might want to read it."

While he returned to typing in two-fingered fashion, Jill sat down to read the editorial. The heading was: ARE YOU A GOOD CITIZEN?

The editorial was really a series of questions: Do you know the names of your local, state and nationally elected officials? Do you know their records? Do you know the stand they take on various issues? Do you know conditions in Mapleville—schools, hospitals, sanitation, fire protection, health protection? It ended with a few curt words of comment: If you don't know the answers you are a bad citizen. Isn't it time you remembered that the government is you?"

Loomis ripped a page out of the machine and yelled, "Harry!" He clipped sheets together and handed them to the boy who came in. Then he turned to smile at Jill.

"Well?" he asked. "Have you picked up any ideas?"

She nodded eagerly. "I'll ask the governors for permission to use the Institute for an evening every two weeks for meetings. We could rent chairs from the funeral parlor. What we need is to import one famous speaker a month and for the alternate meeting have a prominent local speaker."

"Bringing in big people will cost a lot," Loomis warned.

"I'm sure the governors will consent to my financing that part of it."

"What makes you think people will come?" he asked.

"We'll make the meetings so interesting that they won't be able to stay away. And," Jill's eyes sparkled, "you'll be the local speaker for the first meeting."

"The deuce I will! I'm an editor, gal, not a speaker."

"But you know more about Mapleville, as a whole, than anyone else. You could tell them what's wrong."

Loomis chuckled. "They won't like that."

"And then goad them into a debate to find out how to make things better."

"You want to see the fur fly, don't you."

"I just want Mapleville to stay beautiful and peaceful. You don't need to point out just the bad things. Remember how the people got together to paint the Robinsons' house when Mr. Robinson was paralyzed? And how—"

"Okay, gal, I've got the picture. Your job is to get to work on the governors while I see what kind of ideas I can dig up."

As Jill started for the door, the editor called sharply, "Hey, gal, come back."

His eyes raked her face. "Look here, Abraham Allen is one of the governors of the Institute, isn't he?"

Jill nodded.

"Was this his idea?" She shook her head, but he wasn't satisfied. "You sure he didn't sort of plant the idea with you?"

"I'm perfectly sure. In fact, Chester Bennett warned me this morning that Mr. Allen doesn't like the idea of me stirring people up."

"I can take your word," the editor said. "You can't lie with eyes like that. I just wondered. Allen's an ambitious man and he'd do a lot to be elected Senator. But if he's not behind this there's a chance he could try to prevent it."

"That," Jill said coolly, "would be very foolish of Mr. Allen. Once people found out that he was trying to prevent open discussion—"

Loomis chuckled. "I guess you can handle Honest Abe." He sobered. "At least I hope you can. He could be a bad enemy."

"So I've been told," Jill said. "But, as it says in the history books, I'll fight it out on this line if it takes all summer."

IX

"Now," Mrs. Meam said, "you put the lobster into the boiling water."

There was a moment's flushed struggle and then Jill said, "Ugh!"

Mrs. Meam laughed. "You'll get used to it."

"What do we do now?"

The older woman poured coffee and took crisp fresh rolls out of the oven.

As she buttered the third one, Jill sighed with repletion. "I always seem to be eating when I'm in this house."

"It's good for you."

"What ever happened—" Jill began while her courage was high. It failed. "—to your lodger?"

"Now that's a funny thing." The older woman frowned in perplexity. "Peter Carr waited here that day to have a talk with him.

94

He waited hours but John Jones never came back."

"Maybe he was afraid. What did he say when he did return?"

"But that's what I mean, child. My lodger never came back at all. At least —"

Slowly Jill set her cup back on its saucer, her eyes wide with surprise. "Not at all? Aunt Sally, you mean you've never seen him since then?"

"Not so much as to lay eyes on him."

"This," Jill said slowly, "is the queerest story I ever heard."

"It has me puzzled," Mrs. Meam admitted.

"Maybe," Jill suggested, "he was afraid of Peter Carr."

Queer how difficult she found it to say his name without embarrassment, and yet how much she wanted to say his name.

"But according to the stories you both told me, he had left the warehouse before — Peter Carr got there."

"That's right. Well, I just don't understand it. The mystery of the missing lodger."

"Right now," Mrs. Meam said briskly, "we must concentrate on the mystery of the boiled lobster."

Sometime later, when the cooking lesson was over, Jill said, "Aunt Sally, I've been wondering about your lodger. Have you looked in his room to see if you could find out anything about him?"

"Oh, yes. I cleared it out. By the way, I got a new lodger that very day but I put her in the east room. You never can tell, the Jones man might come back. I don't much like women lodgers, as a rule. They are too fussy and they expect to be waited on or to use my kitchen to make tea or something, but I just can't afford to turn down anyone who wants to rent a room when I get the chance."

"What a pity, with all your hard work you weren't able to put aside any money."

"I put it aside all right," Mrs. Meam said. "A nice little nest egg. I could have made out on it but —"

"You lost it?"

"I plunged the whole thing in phony oil stock."

"Oh, Aunt Sally!"

"And yet I don't feel half as bad over being mistaken in the investment as I do about being mistaken in the man who cheated me, and that's a fact. Andrew Trevor was the nicest man I ever knew. A widower with one son. Fine to work for. I was his housekeeper. And he did more for this town than anyone." She added with a defiant note in her voice, "And

I stick to that no matter what anyone may say and no matter what he may have done afterwards."

Jill gave a little gurgle of laughter. "They were talking about him last night at the Bennetts' dinner party. Mr. Clayton seemed to feel the way you do, but Mr. Allen—"

Mrs. Meam sniffed. "Honest Abe! He was so jealous of Mr. Trevor and the way people felt about him that he could hardly stand it. Talk about the green-eyed monster! He has always wanted to be first in this town and now that Mr. Trevor's gone he has his chance. Between you and me, he was the only one in Mapleville who was downright pleased when Andrew Trevor was publicly disgraced."

"What became of him?"

"Mr. Trevor? He was right sick and he went West somewhere to get back his health. That's all I know. No one ever heard a word after that."

"And his son? It must have been awful for him, knowing his father was disgraced."

"Yes, I suppose so," Mrs. Meam said vaguely, "though, if you ask me, he was so crazy in love with Denise Clayton that he didn't have one thought out of five to give to his poor father." She began to polish the already spotless table. "Queer goings on," she

97

said in a puzzled voice. "It gets so you don't know for sure what to believe."

She looked up as a shadow fell across the screen door.

"May I come in?" It was Peter Carr's quiet voice and Jill's heart lurched. From where she sat she could not see him and she realized that he was not aware of her presence. He hadn't come on her account.

"Yes, Mr. Carr," Mrs. Meam said quickly, almost—almost like a warning, Jill thought.

He opened the door and came in, taking a swift look around. His face lighted up when he saw her.

"Miss Bellamy! Hello, there. No more disturbances?"

"Not one," she assured him. She held out her hand. "I haven't really thanked you for your great kindness to me."

He held her hand in a firm warm grasp, gray eyes smiling down at her. Then he turned to Mrs. Meam, who was watching them with a troubled expression on her kindly face.

"Somehow I always head for the kitchen. I hope you don't mind."

"N-no," she said slowly.

"I was wondering if you had heard any more about your mysterious lodger."

98

She shook her head. "Unless he was the one who was here in the night—and I think he was."

"Last night?"

Mrs. Meam nodded grimly. "About two in the morning. Something woke me up and I heard someone walking around upstairs. I sleep in that little room on the first floor. Well, I thought it might be Miss Thompkins—"

"Miss Thompkins?" Peter asked sharply.

"My new lodger. Miss Lola Thompkins. And more Lola than Thompkins, if you ask me. Half Spanish. Then I could tell the noise was in the west room, the one John Jones had. I thought maybe he'd come back. But I didn't want to alarm my new lodger so I didn't call out. I went upstairs."

"Mrs. Meam!" Carr protested.

"Well, someone had to do it," she said practically, "and I wasn't going to just lie there and let someone rob my house."

"Well?" Jill prodded her breathlessly.

"Well, sure enough, there was a flashlight moving around the room. I saw a suitcase on the floor. So I said, keeping my voice down on account of Miss Thompkins, 'Who are you and what are you doing here?' and someone gasped. The flashlight went out and then someone rushed past me, down the stairs and out the front door.

"I turned on the light and the suitcase was gone. Everything belonging to John Jones had been cleared out. So if it wasn't my lodger, who was it?"

"But how did he get in?" Carr asked, puzzled.

"I give my lodgers keys and he hadn't returned his."

"Well—" Carr drew a long breath—"that's quite a story. What does the local trooper have to say?"

"I haven't told him." There was a shade of defiance in Mrs. Meam's voice. "There's no cause. He left money for his rent. And anyhow, it might scare my new lodger."

"What might scare your new lodger, Mrs. Meam?" The voice that asked the question was a rich contralto. The girl crossed the dining room with a click of high heels. Her white dress contrasted dramatically with the sheen of coal-black hair.

"This is my new lodger, Miss Lola Thompkins," Mrs. Meam said. "Miss Bellamy. Mr. Carr."

The Spanish girl summed up Jill in a swift look, dismissed her with a mechanical smile and passed on to the tall young man with the

100

steady gray eyes.

"Mr. Carr?" she purred.

His face seemed like granite. The gray eyes were as expressionless as glass. "How do you do, Miss Thompkins."

The girl gave him a long look, turned back to scrutinize Jill. Then she repeated her first question. "And what might scare your new lodger, Mrs. Meam?"

"There's been some talk about housebreaking," Mrs. Meam answered truthfully if obliquely.

The Spanish girl laughed. Her magnificent dark eyes sparkled. Her head was tilted in a kind of bravado. "I am not easily scared."

Carr was watching her gravely. There was no particular expression on his face, but Jill knew that he was furiously angry. The girl knew it, too, and she was entertained.

"I must go," Jill said quickly. "I hope you'll enjoy your stay in Mapleville, Miss Thompkins."

"It should be interesting."

"Do you expect to be here long?"

Lola Thompkins made a vague gesture. "I have no idea. It depends on how things work out."

Jill smiled and nodded and went out, hoping that Peter Carr would suggest walking home with her, but the Spanish girl exclaimed, "A hammock. Do come out in the shade and talk to me, Mr. Carr."

"With pleasure," he said politely.

Jill walked off, head high, her cheeks flushing. What was wrong with Peter Carr? He hadn't come near her, hadn't called her. It couldn't be because he thought he would not be welcome. She had made her liking for him obvious. Much too obvious.

Then why? Was it because of this Spanish girl? No, he'd just met her and he didn't seem to like her. Yet he had said "With pleasure" when she asked him to stay with her.

But there was no pleasure in his face as he watched Jill walk swiftly down the street. With a stony face he followed Lola Thompkins out onto the lawn.

"Well?" she challenged him.

"Why did you come here, Lola?"

She looked at his angry face. "Just chance."

"Chance nothing! Why? How did you know where I was?"

"Don't be cross, darling!"

"How did you know where I was?" he repeated.

"I dropped in to see your father and there happened to be a letter from you lying on the

102

table in plain sight. I recognized your writing, though the name with the return address was Peter Carr. So I thought I would come East and take a look at this man Carr."

"Well?"

She lay back in the hammock, studying his face through half-closed eyes.

"You're up to something, Jim," she said at length.

"It doesn't concern you, Lola," he said in a level voice. "I don't want you to interfere."

"No?" There was a slow smile on her full lips.

"No," he said grimly.

"Are you going to tell me about it?"

"No."

She sat up abruptly. "I intend to find out."

He stretched out his hand and caught her wrist. "This isn't a game. You might cause more trouble than you could even imagine. What good would that do?"

She smiled at him and unexpectedly he remembered a beautiful long-haired black cat he had had as a child. A lovely cat with a magnificent coat and amber eyes. A cat as soft as silk to touch. But, without warning, claws sprang in the velvet paws and dug abruptly into a small boy's trusting hand, leaving deep scratches and drawing blood.

"I always knew," she said, "that there was a girl you'd left behind you. A girl you couldn't forget. You made that quite clear, Jim."

He made no reply.

"Very clear," she repeated softly. "We've been good friends, we've had wonderful times together, there have been moments when you—almost—forgot her with me. But never altogether."

He looked down at her, as remote as the Old Man of the Mountain. A man of granite. Unreachable.

"Is that Bellamy girl the one you were so mad about?"

"No," he said at length, "she's not the one."

She stood up and put her hand gently on his arm. "Can't you even pretend to be glad to see me, Jim?" she said wistfully. "I've come a long way. Won't you at least take me to dinner?"

"Lola, you don't understand my position here. You might find it awkward, to say the least, to dine publicly with me. It could be very embarrassing for you."

She looked at him thoughtfully. "I'll risk it. Tomorrow night? There's an inn here with dancing on Thursday nights. Please, darling."

"Of course," he said with formal politeness. "I'll make reservations at once. Shall I pick you up at seven? I'm sorry that I haven't a car of my own here but—"

"What! Jim Trevor without a car!" She laughed. "Well, I've rented one." She added almost sharply, "For a month. You can drive that. Tomorrow at seven, then."

X

Peter Carr turned off the motor and went back to open the door. Clayton got out and gave a hand to Denise, who followed him. As she had done from the beginning, she gave the chauffeur a quick malicious look and then went into the house without any acknowledgement of his existence.

"That's all, Peters," Clayton said in his big, carrying voice. "You won't be needed again tonight."

"Very well, sir," the chauffeur answered colorlessly.

Clayton dropped his voice. "Anything to report?"

"I hope to have something more concrete after tonight."

"Nothing — new?"

"The man John Jones seems to have disappeared from his rooming house."

Clayton looked at the tall man in his trim uniform and the look was returned steadily. The older man was troubled. The gangling boy whom he vaguely remembered from four summers ago had become a mature man. He had a fine and intelligent face. Anyone who underrated him would be a fool. Perhaps this idea of having him masquerade as a chauffeur had not been very smart.

The young man himself gave no indication of how he felt. He was acting entirely in accordance with the original agreement. Nonetheless, Clayton was aware that Denise was getting a good deal of amusement out of giving the new chauffeur peremptory orders. There had, Clayton suspected, been a time when Trevor—Peters, he corrected himself —had been attracted to his daughter. If he was right, her manner must be a constant humiliation to a man who was only doing the job he had been asked to do.

Clayton sighed. He had probably spoiled Denise. Certainly other people had spoiled her. She was so pretty that all her life people had made a fuss over her, flattered her, praised her beauty. But that didn't excuse her behavior now. And it certainly wasn't Peters alone who had felt her malice. She had barely pretended to be friendly with Gillian Bellamy.

Though that, her father was shrewdly aware, was because Gillian was equally lovely and had a far greater fortune.

Well, things would probably work out. Denise was too old to take orders from him and Peters was mature and self-controlled enough to take her rudeness in his stride.

"Yes—well, I agreed not to interfere," he said heavily. "But if you should want to call on me for anything—"

"Thank you, sir."

Peter Carr drove the car into the garage and climbed the stairs to his own room. He stripped off the uniform, dressed in dark slacks, sweater and sneakers, and Jim Trevor went to look out of the window. With a pair of binoculars he scanned the Bennett place next door, its terrace clearly visible by the light spilling out from windows. They were all having highballs on the lawn except Jill, who had her usual glass of lemonade. Dan Holt was curled up at her feet, talking, and Chester Bennett watched the couple with a somber expression.

Jim put down the binoculars. Gillian Bellamy was safe for the time being. Indeed, he was inclined to doubt that there would be any more "accidents." Too much attention had been attracted to the things that had already happened to her. The man who had engineered them must be aware of the risk he would run in provoking another attack on the girl.

Jim sat down to write a report to Mr. Garrison. Ever since Gillian Bellamy had told him of the missing bust by Praxiteles there had been the stirring of an idea in his mind. He unscrewed his fountain pen, stared blankly at the paper and then laid down his pen. His mind was not on the report he had to make. It was preoccupied with three girls.

For four years Denise Clayton, his first love, had been an obsession with him. He had been head over heels in love with her. The fact that she had hurt him intolerably had not affected his feelings for the exquisite golden girl. In all that time no other woman had been able to stir his pulse.

In Oklahoma, where he had visited his father the year before, he had met Lola Thompkins, daughter of a Spanish mother and a Yankee father, a fascinating blend of two different cultures. Lola had the smoldering fire of her Spanish mother and the shrewdness of her Yankee father. The two young people had been thrown together a great deal in the Southwest, where his father had spectacularly recouped his fortune, and Jim had found her a pleasant and most alluring companion. Knowing that Denise was lost to him, he had tried to persuade himself that he was in love with Lola. Failing that, he had told himself that love did not matter. Lola would make him an agreeable and attractive wife.

That she was more than willing to marry him he was honest enough to admit to himself, but there were times when he wondered how much of her interest was aroused by his father's sudden wealth and how much by Jim Trevor himself.

In the long run, he had discovered that the prospect of a loveless marriage, however suitable it might be, chilled him, and he had left for New York after an evening with Lola in which he had tried to make clear that he had no intentions where she was concerned.

At the prospect of seeing Denise again every thought of Lola had been wiped out of his memory. The moment when Denise had emerged from the shadowed doorway of the Plaza into the sunlight was still etched sharply on his mind. He had stood beside the open door of the car, stiff and erect in his new uniform, his face passive, his heart thudding. She had given him one swift look and then stepped into the car without a word.

For a moment Jim had been unbearably

tempted to walk away and return to the law firm to submit his resignation. It was the thought of his father that had restrained him.

Since then, something odd, something totally unexpected had happened to him. Day by day, he had observed Denise covertly. Lovely? She certainly was. As pretty a girl as he had ever seen. But—had the big blue eyes always been so shallow? Had the red lips always been so malicious? Had the small hands always been so greedy? Within a few days he awakened one morning with a sense of deliverance. He was free of Denise. She could never inflict pain on him again.

The unexpected thing had happened the day he went prowling around the warehouse to see whether there was anything to substantiate the Bellamy girl's story that someone had hurled rocks at her and caused her to plunge into the river. He had heard a girl's terrified scream, heard her frantic cry for help. He had hurled himself at the door, breaking it open, and dragged her out into the sunlight.

He had looked at the shining auburn hair, at the tender mouth, at the wide honest eyes and thought, with a shock of recognition, "I've found her." In that dazed moment he had tried to reason with himself. Love at first sight? Ridiculous. It doesn't happen in real life. We're not Romeo and Juliet, who met and loved when they had barely exchanged fifty words. And the girl had said, in a shaken, wondering tone, protesting as he was protesting, "Juliet?"

It had required all his self-control to let the moment pass. And she was Gillian Bellamy, the girl he had been sent to protect. She was also, according to Denise, engaged to marry Chester Bennett.

Jim pounded his right fist into his left hand. Well, what could he expect? Did he imagine that a girl like that, beautiful, simple, honest, gallant, gay of heart, would not be snatched up? He had to stand aside. And yet —and yet—she had said "Juliet" in that breathless way.

He took a long breath. Whether he could ever tell her how he felt about her did not matter now. What did matter was that the accidents had really happened. Three times Gillian Bellamy had been in danger. The fourth time, when he had found her locked in the warehouse—what had *They* intended to do?

That brought him to John Jones, Mrs. Meam's mysterious lodger, who had disappeared from the warehouse and later from the Meam house. But what had the man Jones been doing at the warehouse? On his own hasty inspection trip through the building, while Jill waited outside, he had seen a number of packing cases on the first floor. He remembered that they had each had a queer mark: ϕ. On the second floor there had been a padlocked door which he had been unable to open.

Tonight, he was going to examine every foot of the building and find out what it was being used for. He looked at the tools he had collected: screwdriver, chisel, crowbar. He added a flashlight. He glanced at his watch. Only eleven o'clock. He'd wait at least another two hours. These warm summer nights people went to bed late. Better give them time to fall sound asleep before he set off.

Once more he adjusted the binoculars. Dan Holt was returning to the Clayton house. The Bennetts and Gillian were going inside, Chester walking with Gillian, his arm around her. He said something and they both laughed. The Bennetts followed, obviously pleased with the young people's absorption in each other.

When the Bennetts had disappeared into their own house, Jim went back to his desk to write the report. The accidents, he related, were authentic. They had obviously been engineered. That meant someone wanted to eliminate Gillian Bellamy. Because they had come in quick succession, it seemed apparent that someone was in a hurry, that something must happen to the Bellamy girl before she was twenty-one.

The people who would profit by her death were William Bennett, Abraham Allen and Roger Clayton. Clayton had been in New York at the time of the first three accidents. This appeared to remove him as a suspect. But did it? After all, it might be an attempt to establish an alibi. The man who had engineered the attacks on Miss Bellamy need not have been on the scene. This fellow John Jones could be, and probably was, the active agent.

Jim suggested that the law firm check in New York on the financial standing of all three men. Then he sat tapping his pen on the table, frowning. Roger Clayton was not the only governor with an alibi. At the time when someone had hurled rocks at Gillian Bellamy, William Bennett and Abraham Allen had been together. Or had they? This was something else to check on.

Abraham Allen. Honest Abe. For a moment Jim Trevor's good-looking face lost its easy-going quality, grew hard as granite. So far, he had not laid eyes on Honest Abe, but he intended to do so. It was Abe Allen to whom his father had written, expressing his desire to make full restitution of the money his former neighbors had lost through their investments in oil. It was Abe Allen who had replied tartly that the people of Mapleville wanted no further dealings with Andrew Trevor.

But—and this was what made hot anger lick along Jim's veins—Abraham Allen had never told the people of Mapleville about Trevor's offer. In the interview he had had with Mrs. Meam, his father's old housekeeper, while he waited in vain for John Jones to return, Jim had discovered the truth.

Honest Abe indeed! Sooner or later, Jim intended to settle his father's score with Abraham Allen and force Allen to admit publicly that Andrew Trevor was willing to make full restitution of the money that had been lost because of the trust his friends and neighbors had in him.

Jim finished his report. For the first time he realized that no lights showed in the village. Time for him to be on his way.

He lay in the long grass and looked at the

warehouse. He had overlooked the one thing he most needed—his binoculars. Something was going on. Garrison had warned him that he was not to appear publicly in the matter, so he watched from his vantagepoint.

A big torch moved around inside the warehouse. Now and then, from its position, he realized that the torch was resting on the floor. Several times a dark shadow moved in front of it but it was impossible to recognize the dim figure. So far as he could make out, the shadow was stooping, lifting something.

Then the light swung in a big arc and went out. The intruder was out of doors now. At intervals there was a heavy thud and a rattle. Then a sound he could not mistake—the slam of a car door. A motor throbbed into life, lights were switched on. He lay flat as the car backed and turned, the lights sweeping over the long grass and weeds. Then they were gone and he leaped to his feet. A small pickup truck was moving rapidly toward the village.

He hesitated, torn between two courses of action. He could try to follow the truck on foot and get the license number, or he could follow his original plan and search the warehouse. If it weren't too late. Chances were that someone had forestalled him by removing all traces of the purpose for which the warehouse had been used.

He ducked down out of sight as the truck turned and avoided the searching fingers of the lights as they crept through the weeds. Then the truck was gone and it was dark again.

Too late. He'd never catch up with the truck now. He examined the door. This time it had been carefully locked. He could break it open, of course, but in doing so he would be issuing a warning that he was on the trail. Instead, he took the screwdriver and set to work to remove the hinges.

The job took longer than he had expected. Carefully he lifted the door aside and slipped in. For a moment he stood listening. There was no sound but the slithering of rats. He flashed on his light and began a slow search of the first floor. As he had anticipated, the crates and boxes were gone. At the end of a half hour he had gone over every foot of space. There were no signs of occupancy except in the small office, its door splintered, in which Gillian had been imprisoned.

Here, on the floor, there were excelsior, wood shavings, crumpled paper, two empty boxes. Someone had been in a hurry to remove the evidence. If only, he thought, raging at himself, he hadn't been so stupid! If only he had examined them more closely, looked to see whether there was any indication of their contents, any sign of where they had come from, where they were going.

No use crying over spilt milk, he told himself sharply. Get on with it. He ran up the stairs. The warehouse seemed to extend forever, dark, cavernous, echoing weirdly with his footsteps. He went at once to the padlocked door he had seen on his first trip. Once more he decided to remove the hinges. He worked quickly this time. The hinges were oiled, the metal new, like the big padlock.

Footsteps again. Jim listened, holding his breath. There had been no sound of a motor. Was it the man with the truck who had returned on foot, or was it someone else? In any case, the man would know he was there. The door off its hinges would provide plenty of warning.

He snapped off his flashlight and stood motionless. In sneakers he moved almost soundlessly. He tried to remember the layout of the second floor, the location of the stairs. There was no place to hide here. He didn't want to be cut off from any means of escape.

The footsteps below were cautious. He gripped the big chisel and fastened his flash-

light to his belt. There was a gleam of light coming up the stairwell. At once he oriented himself and he crept noiselessly, careful step by careful step, hoping he could avoid creaking boards. If he could only get a look at the fellow!

Then someone began to climb the stairs while he backed away toward the wall. The feet stopped abruptly. The other man was listening as he was listening. The feet retreated.

What was he doing down there? At last the man below made up his mind. He was moving fast now, making no attempt to conceal his movements. He walked from end to end of the building. But what—what in heaven's name—was he up to? There was nothing left downstairs. Nothing at all.

There was the sound of paper being crumpled up. Then an odd sound as though someone had knocked over a bucket of water. A pungent smell filled the air. Gasoline?

There was a flicker of light. More light. The stairwell was as bright as day. A roar of sound.

Fire!

For a moment Jim stood stock-still, horrified by the leaping flames. Then he turned quickly, seeking some means of escape. There was no possibility of going down the stairs. They were already a flaming mass. No chance of surviving that inferno.

Already smoke was billowing up, blinding him, making him choke. The floor under his sneakers was uncomfortably hot. The building, made of dry wood, was like tinder. Once the fire started there would be no controlling it.

Don't panic, he told himself sharply. It's panic that kills people more often than the fire itself. Panic—and smoke. Steady now. Think out what you've got to do.

He had backed away from the stairwell until he was pressed against the outer wall. With his chisel he smashed a window pane and let in the fresh air. He gulped it in gratefully. In the distance he heard a hoarse hooting sound, the fire alarm in the village. But would they come in time?

He noticed that the fire seemed to be confined to one side of the building. The side he was on! The side where, on the second floor, there was a padlocked door behind which something was hidden, something so revealing that it had to be destroyed.

If he could get across to the other side he'd have a chance. He forced himself to study the position. How could he cross that blazing stairwell? If he could get around it some way —

He looked up and saw the rafters. There was a chance. A slim one but a chance. He stepped on the windowsill, clutched and clawed at a small projection on the wall, and then stretched up until his fingers touched the rafter above him. He braced himself and then jumped up. His right hand reached up, caught on the rafter. Then his left hand. He swung there. How far apart were they? Carefully he measured the distance. Then, holding on with his left hand, he swung himself as far as he could, grabbing for the next rafter. Missed! It seemed to him as though he had almost wrenched his left arm out of its socket.

He tried again. Made it! Cautiously, one by one, he swung from rafter to rafter. He was directly above the stairwell now, looking down into an inferno. The heat seemed to sear his face. He was across it, moving away, toward the far end of the warehouse. Once something furry touched his hand and he nearly fell. An escaping rat had lodged on the rafter beside him.

He was beyond the immediate range of the flames now. He let himself drop onto the floor. He felt the jolt from the soles of his feet right through his skull. The air was thick now, unbreathable. Smoke billowed around him, choking him. He dragged himself toward a window, tried to pull it up, tried to break the glass. His arms moved without strength, make a feeble tap, dropped listlessly to his side.

You can't give up, he told himself fiercely. There's no one to look after Jill. You can't give up.

On hands and knees he crawled up to the window. The air seemed fresher against the floor. For a moment he rested his cheek against it, felt his eyes close. He dragged himself up again, struck the window pane. The tap was so light it didn't even crack the glass. He set his teeth, swung harder. The glass broke, showering him. He sat up, breathing in great gulps of fresh air, his vision clearing.

There was a turmoil down below, the sickening wail of fire engines, the blinking of red lights, shouts as men maneuvered hoses into position.

He cleared the glass away cautiously with his hand, covered by part of his sweater, and looked down.

A girl's voice rose, above the confusion, a voice he would have known anywhere. "Look! Up there! Get him out! Get him out!"

It was Gillian Bellamy. It seemed to him as

though new life had stirred in his smoke-dulled body. A ladder swayed, came to rest near the window. He looked out. Down below, his face drawn and white, Chester Bennett held the ladder.

"Can you make it?" he called. "If not, I'll get someone to hold this and come up for you. I can't get it any closer to the window."

"I'll make it." He looked out. The ladder was several feet to the left of the window. He got out onto the windowsill, judged the distance carefully, and then, with a long easy swing, he caught the ladder.

For a sickening moment it swayed dangerously and then it settled firmly against the wall. He swarmed down it.

Chester Bennett was still holding it in place. Sweat was pouring down his face.

"I guess I owe you my life," Jim said.

There was a crash, a reverberation that shook the ground, a shower of sparks. The far end of the warehouse had fallen in.

XI

Something awakened Jill and she sat bolt up-right in bed, her heart thudding. There it was again, the ominous rising and falling sound of a siren. Outside the window the sky was as light as day, but a queer red.

Fire!

She looked at her bedside clock. Nearly four in the morning. She tumbled out of bed and ran to the window. Cars were starting up, people were calling questions. In the house below, there were voices, people moving around.

She flung open the door and called, "Where is it?" Her voice rose in a panic. "Not the Institute?"

"We can't tell yet," Mrs. Bennett called back. "I wish you would go to bed, child."

"Where are Chester and Mr. Bennett?"

"They've gone to the fire, though I begged

William to stay here."

"I'm going, too."

"No, Gillian. I won't permit it. You aren't strong."

Jill went back into her room to pull on dark slacks and a short-sleeved blouse. At the door she hesitated. Mrs. Bennett was in the living room below. She'd never let her go. Only rarely did she attempt to exert her authority, but when she did so she was adamant. But if the fire should be at the Institute—

Jill stole quietly down the back stairs. Then, setting her lips, she returned to her room, hunted for her car keys. Time she made herself drive again and it would save at least a quarter of an hour. Chester had kept the car in shape for her. Only the day before, he had checked the battery and tires and had the tank filled with gas.

In the garage she started the car, let it warm up, and then backed down the sloping driveway, hoping that Mrs. Bennett would not hear her. On the road she switched on lights and waited until another fire truck went by with wailing siren.

If it was the Institute burning—but surely the building was fireproofed. Every precaution had been taken in its construction, and there was a night watchman.

She was nearer now. The sky was bright with its ominous red glow. A car passed her, then another. The village was turning out. Practically all the able-bodied men were volunteer firemen, she remembered.

They were turning to the right now. Why — it was the warehouse! She parked the car, pocketed her keys and began to run. The fire seemed to be at one end of the warehouse. The whole thing was in a blaze. As she watched, horrified, flames shot up through the roof.

The other end was untouched as yet, though through the windows she could see flickering lights. There were ladders and hoses and shouting men. She began to make out faces. Roger Clayton was wielding an ax. Dan Holt was one man on a hose. Mr. Bennett was watching, his face too high in color.

Then someone shouted, "Keep back, you fool!" and dragged Abraham Allen away from the door of the blazing building.

Allen shook off the restraining hands. "There's someone inside. Second floor."

"You won't help him by getting killed yourself. Keep back, Allen!" Strong hands dragged the resisting man back by main force.

Jill looked up, aghast. No one could be in

there. No one could live in that inferno. Then there was a crash of breaking glass as a window was splintered. A man leaned out, cautious of jagged glass. It was Peter Carr.

For a moment Jill's heart was cold with horror. Then she screamed, "Look! Up there! Get him out! Get him out!"

There was a rush of men led by Chester; a ladder tilted, rested against the wall.

Jill had a vague impression of a crash, a roar of flames. The roof at the other end of the warehouse had caved in. She thought she saw a shower of sparks explode like fireworks against the sky and then it was dark. Dark and hot, so hot she could not bear it. Searing heat. Out of the darkness a voice said, "Jill! Jill! Darling, are you all right? Oh, my dearest, if anything's happened to you—"

Arms gathered her up, carried her away from the heat, away from the shouting voices. She opened her eyes. Peter Carr, blood running down his cheek from a cut, his face smeared with soot, was looking at her.

"Peter?"

He set her gently on her feet but his arms still held her. She clutched at his shirt with both hands, clung to him, shaking. The world whirled around her, straightened again.

One arm drew her close, a gentle hand probed lightly at her head. She winced.

"I fell," she said. "I guess. I don't remember."

"Someone slugged you in the confusion," he said, his voice tight and hard. "Shoved you against the building."

"Left me to burn?" It was a whisper.

Peter made no answer.

"How did you find me?"

"I heard your voice when I broke open the window."

"How could you possibly hear me in all that noise?"

"I'd hear your voice whisper if it was on the other side of the world."

"But how did you find me?"

"I hunted everywhere. In those few seconds I lived years." He lifted her chin, bent over and kissed her mouth.

When he released her it seemed to Jill that the whole world had changed, had grown radiant and alight. Fire—she turned her head. No, this wasn't another fire. The sun was rising.

Peter's eyes held a message she was not yet prepared to hear. His mouth was tender. "It was the lark and not the nightingale," he said softly.

So he had heard and understood her choked word, "Juliet." He, too, was familiar with the lovely words exchanged by those immortal lovers, Romeo and Juliet.

She turned away, her cheeks burning.

"Where are you going?" he asked.

"My car is over there," she said.

"You drove?" He was surprised. "You weren't afraid?"

"I forgot to be afraid." She added more clearly, "I'll never be afraid of the car again."

"Just the same," he said, holding out his hand for the keys, "I'll drive you home. I don't want you out in the dark alone."

They drove in silence, leaving behind the firefighters, the sound of axes cutting into the warehouse, the smell of burned wood under water.

It's happened again, Jill thought. Someone knocked me out. But why? Why? What have I ever done to make anyone hate me so? And Peter Carr saved me again. *It was the lark and not the nightingale.*

She could still feel the warm pressure of his lips on hers. She hadn't known a kiss could be like that.

Peter Carr leaned forward, frowning at the fuel gauge. "I hope there's enough gas to get you home."

129

"Oh, that's all right," she assured him. "Chester had the car filled for me yesterday, tires and battery checked."

"Are you sure?" he asked in a tone that startled her.

"Why, yes, of course. What's wrong?"

"The tank is registering almost empty."

"That's queer," she said in a puzzled voice.

"Who else drives this car?"

"No one. Peter! Why do you look like that?"

He forced a smile. "No reason at all. That's just my ugly mug you're objecting to."

"You had better tell me," she said quietly. "I can take it."

He gave her a quick look and nodded approval. "I guess you can at that. I think I know where the gas came from."

"What gas?"

"The warehouse fire," he said grimly. "The place was soaked in gasoline. I smelled it. In fact, I heard someone empty a bucket of the stuff just before the building went up in flames."

"My car?" Jill said in a small voice. "Someone who could get at my car. Someone — I know."

His hand covered hers, held it warm and safe.

"Who did it, Peter?" she asked at last.

"I don't know. But I'm going to find out." After a moment he said harshly, "And to think I promised you that it had stopped, that nothing more would happen to you. After this, don't go anywhere alone. Always have someone with you."

"But whom," Jill asked, "can I trust?"

"I don't know," he admitted. "Except for Chester Bennett. He saved my life tonight. A few minutes longer and I'd have had it."

At least, he thought bitterly, I've told her. I owe Chester Bennett that much. And if it's true that she is engaged to him she has a right to know that he did a darned fine thing.

He stopped at the Bennett house. "Will you be all right?"

"Of course. And thank you." She turned to him smiling. Something flamed in his eyes. For a moment she thought he was going to kiss her again. She wanted him to kiss her, to hold her, warm and safe in his arms.

Instead, he opened the door and got out of the car.

"Good night," he said, and he walked quickly away.

Neither of the Bennett cars had returned when Jill got back to the house. Mrs. Bennett

131

had gone up to bed without, apparently, noticing Jill's absence.

In her own room Jill stripped off her clothes and bathed. There was a lump behind her right ear. Her face was streaked with soot. There was a long ugly burn on her left arm. She applied soothing lotion and bandaged it. Before going to bed she stood at the window. The fire had died down. The light that filled the sky now was the dawning of a new day.

It was the lark, she repeated softly to herself.

She got into bed and moved her cheek against the smooth cool pillowslip. Her eyelids closed. She had given herself away completely to Peter Carr—and she didn't care. She knew nothing about him and yet she knew everything that mattered. As she fell asleep her lips quivered, feeling still the warmth of his kiss upon them.

When she awakened it was nearly eleven o'clock. A twinge of pain from the burned arm brought back vivid pictures of the night and the fire, of Peter trapped in the burning building. Of Peter finding her where she had been left to burn to death. Of Peter's voice, passionate in its tenderness, saying, *Oh, my dearest, if anything's happened to you—*

She dressed in a full peasant skirt and a blouse with bishop sleeves that concealed the bandage. The face in the mirror was pale, the eyes shadowed, but the mouth seemed fuller, warmer, softer than before.

When she came downstairs Mrs. Bennett called from the morning room where she made out her menus, wrote letters and paid household bills. "Oh, there you are. I'm glad you had such a good sleep. You certainly don't look well." She rang the bell. "Though how you could sleep through all the confusion—"

She broke off to ask the maid to bring Miss Bellamy's breakfast tray into the morning room.

"We've all had breakfast," she said in a martyred tone when Jill started to protest. "I don't think Chester got to bed at all and poor William had only three hours' sleep. Out until nearly six this morning, and then that man called before he was up. So I had to wake him. They are still talking."

Jill was grateful for the prompt arrival of her breakfast tray, which provided her with an occupation. She poured coffee, put cream on blueberries, and buttered a muffin.

"The warehouse burned down," Mrs. Bennett went on. "I've just been listening to the local radio station. There were fire engines from six towns; nearly eighty people were out fighting the blaze."

"The Institute?" Jill asked quickly.

"Oh, the fire couldn't spread across the river, thank heaven, but from what I hear there's nothing but charred wood left of that old building. And then a wind came up and there were sparks blown for acres through the weeds. Dry as chips they were, too, because we've had no rain. People ran like mad, beating them out with gunny sacks and brooms and whatever they could find. Chester and William were over there for hours, though at William's age I don't think he should exert himself so much. It's bad for his heart. But, of course, it's your property and he feels responsible." She looked at the girl's downcast face. "So does Chester. There's nothing he wouldn't do for you."

This was her chance, Jill thought. She'd tell Mrs. Bennett that she wasn't going to marry Chester.

There were men's voices in the hall. Mr. Bennett came in with a thin, nervously energetic man with a narrow face, observant eyes and a disillusioned mouth.

Jill looked at her guardian in shocked dismay. No wonder Mrs. Bennett had been

134

concerned about her husband's overexertion and lack of rest. His face was crimson, his breathing a loud wheeze; his hands shook violently.

"Here you are, my dear. No, go ahead with your breakfast. This is Mr. Hartman. My ward, Miss Bellamy."

Bennett eased himself into a chair and waved his guest toward another. Hartman sat down and took a look at the room that was like an inventory. His eyes then went to Mrs. Bennett, summed her up in a quick glance, passed on to Jill.

"I'm from the International Insurance Company, Miss Bellamy. We handle your fire insurance. Luckily I was in Mapleville on another case, so I was right on the spot when that warehouse fire broke out last night."

Jill nodded and finished the blueberries. She poured more coffee.

Bennett wheezed. "I'm afraid there's some trouble, Gillian. I explained to Mr. Hartman that you don't control any of the business of your estate—in fact, you can't until you are twenty-one—but he insisted on seeing you."

Again Jill nodded without speaking. Something about the insurance man's expression when he looked at her was disturbing. What a horrible life, she thought; imagine having to

135

spend your days looking at people because you suspect them of doing something wrong. Ugh!

Hartman said easily, "I always like to go to headquarters. In the long run, it saves my time. Now, Miss Bellamy, it's the way your guardian here has told you. I check insurance claims just in case there's any hanky-panky. Well, I found it here, all right. The fire that destroyed your warehouse last night was deliberately set."

She remembered the missing gasoline from her car. How much should she tell this man? "Why," she asked, "would anyone burn down a deserted, tumbledown building? I was going to have it torn down anyhow."

"You were?" He cocked a surprised eyebrow.

She told him about her plan to have the land transformed into gardens.

"Then you do have something to say about the way your property is handled," he commented oddly. "Did you see that fire yourself last night, Miss Bellamy?"

"Of course not," Mrs. Bennett put in before Jill could speak. "I sent her right back to bed. The child's too delicate to be running to fires at all hours of the night."

Gillian bent over to pick up a handkerchief

she had dropped. As she raised her arm the wide sleeve of her blouse fell back. She saw the speculative look in the insurance investigator's eyes as they rested on the bandage. He started to mention it, changed his mind.

"Well—" he got up slowly—"I won't keep you longer now. We'll have to make a complete investigation, of course. You're sure, Mr. Bennett, that the warehouse was not being used for anything?"

Bennett shook his head. "There were some odds and ends of stuff we never got around to disposing of after the Institute was completed. Practically all junk, I'd say. As a matter of fact, we were going to take a careful look at the place in a day or two. Just hadn't gotten around to it."

Mr. Hartman sat down again. "You were? Why?"

"Just tidying up. I don't like loose ends."

"Did you mention your intention to anyone?"

"Why, I don't know. It didn't seem important. Probably the other governors. And my son, of course."

"You spoke of it at dinner, William," his wife reminded him.

"And there was John Jones," Jill said quickly. "He was hanging around the place.

He was busy at something upstairs. I'm sure he was."

"Who is that?" Hartman asked.

Bennett sighed. "Now, Gillian, my dear—"

"Let her tell me in her own way," Hartman said, and at the authoritative note in his voice Bennett subsided.

Jill told the insurance man about John Jones, who had thrown rocks at her and sent her plunging into the river, who had been with the man who locked her in the office, who had disappeared in the night from Mrs. Sally Meam's house. Even as she told it, she realized, with a sinking heart, how improbable the whole story sounded, and her voice dwindled off uncertainly.

"Perhaps," Bennett said, "you won't need to keep my ward any longer, Mr. Hartman. She looks to me like a pretty tired girl and it upsets her, makes her fanciful. All these dreadful things that keep happening to her."

Hartman's shrewd eyes went from Jill's face to her bandaged arm.

"Of course not. I'm on my way. And thanks for being so helpful and cooperative. Good morning, Mrs. Bennett. Good-by for now, Mr. Bennett. Miss Bellamy—" his eyes twinkled as he looked at her—"have you tried First Aid Cream for burns? It's a big help."

He went out, leaving her staring after him. When the outside door had closed, Mrs. Bennett said to her husband, "I wish you'd lie down for a while."

Bennett sat heavily on the couch. "Too much exercise last night for an old man."

Not an old man, Jill thought, but a sick man. A very sick man.

"Let me call your doctor," she said impulsively. "He might be able to do something to make you feel better. Anyhow, you haven't had a checkup in a terribly long time."

"Please do, William," his wife urged him. "I'm really worried about you."

"Nothing a doctor can do to help. I'm just tired."

Tired and sick at heart, Jill thought. But why? The Bennetts had a good life. What was wrong?

XII

A few hours later, she felt that she knew the answer and she was more bewildered than ever. What worried William Bennett, what had made him ill, was his son Chester.

"Where is the boy?" he grumbled fretfully when Chester did not appear at lunchtime.

His wife flashed a quick, triumphant look at Jill. "He was swimming over at the Claytons' pool this morning with Denise. I suppose they kept him for lunch. They all seem to think the world of him. We won't wait any longer."

Bennett scowled at his plate. "I'll be glad when his vacation is over and he goes back to work."

"I must say, William," his wife said indignantly, "Chester works terribly hard all year. He has earned every scrap of his vacation."

"I know. He's a good boy. A hard worker.

I'll always regret he wouldn't go into partnership with me. By now he'd have the galleries, and a pleasant income, and a lot more free time of his own, and a chance to go abroad every year. A pleasant life."

"I never knew that," Jill said in surprise. "Why on earth did he refuse?"

Before Bennett could answer, Chester came into the room, his hair still damp from the pool. He slipped into his chair.

"No thanks, Mother, no lunch. But the Claytons don't go in for desserts. Too fattening, or something. I could do with a large piece of hot apple pie and a slice of cheese so big." He spread his hands about a foot apart.

His mother laughed. "How did you guess we were having apple pie?"

"No guesswork about it. I checked with Wilma this morning." Chester grinned at his mother and turned to Jill. "Did I hear you asking questions about me behind my back, Miss Bellamy?" he asked with mock severity.

"Mata Hari in person," she answered gaily. "Listening at keyholes. You seem to have put in a rugged night."

"Not to much purpose, I'm afraid. There's nothing left of the warehouse."

It was then that Jill noticed how closely Bennett was watching his son, with an expression of gravity mixed with sadness.

"At least," Jill said lightly, "it saved us all the trouble of tearing it down."

"There's going to be some trouble over the insurance, though," Bennett said, still watching Chester. "The company's representative was here this morning. He thinks it was arson."

Chester whistled. "Now that's odd. Who would burn down an empty building?" For a moment he met his father's eyes and then he looked away. He pushed back his chair. "On second thought, I'll take a raincheck on that pie. Will you excuse me, Mother—Jill? I've got some things to do this afternoon and we are dancing at the inn tonight. Remember?"

"Of course," Jill said, trying to sound more enthusiastic than she felt, trying to lift the cloud that had settled over the luncheon table, with Chester and his father eyeing each other warily. "And I have a brand-new dress to wear, so prepare to be dazzled."

It was a white chiffon dress, classically simple in appearance but cut by a great dressmaker and, Jill admitted to herself, wickedly expensive. Nonetheless, as she turned slowly before the mirror that evening, she was glad that she had bought it. It set off perfectly her bare shoulders and arms tanned by the sun, her auburn hair with red lights in it. She covered the burn with a disguising cream so that it was hardly noticeable.

She fastened a small pearl necklace, which had been her mother's, around her slim throat and slid over her shoulders the brief cape of summer ermine which the maid was holding.

"All right?" she said, smiling.

"Beautiful," the maid breathed. "Regal as a queen and dainty as a fairy princess."

Jill laughed. "Gracious!"

Chester was waiting at the foot of the stairs. As Jill came down he made her a low courtly bow and she swept him a deep curtsy. The maid handed her a tiny transparent box in which she saw a gardenia. The card read: *Looking forward to my big evening—Dan.*

She pinned it on her shoulder while Chester stood looking in the mirror at her.

"Perfect," she declared. "Exactly the right flower for this dress."

Chester frowned. "Darn," he said ruefully, "I forgot about flowers for Denise."

Mr. Bennett came out of the living room. "The Queen of Hearts," he declared. "But what is this poor creature with you?" He seemed to have regained his customary good humor.

"The Joker," she laughed, taking Chester's arm.

For a moment Bennett's hand rested lightly on his son's shoulder. "Have fun," he said, "and bring her back safe, Chester."

"Bring 'em back alive," Chester said. "That's my motto. You can trust me for that."

"Yes, I—know." Bennett went heavily back into the living room.

When the outside door had closed behind them, Jill said, "Chester, I'm worried about your father."

"Why?" he asked with a brusqueness that was unusual for him.

"He seems—worried—bothered about something."

"Really, Jill, that imagination of yours is getting out of hand."

"It's not my imagination!" she flared, stung by the amusement in his voice.

"No?"

For a moment she was tempted to tell him that someone had knocked her out the night before and dragged her up against the burning building. She didn't understand herself why she kept silent, why she had kept silent when the insurance man was questioning her. Unless it was because he had so obviously disbelieved what she had told him. And yet she should have informed him that someone had drained the gasoline out of her car in order to start the fire.

They strolled in silence across the expanse of smooth lawn that almost made one estate of the Bennett and Clayton properties. Dan Holt was waiting on the porch for them and he ran down the steps to meet Jill.

"Thank you for the flower," she said. "It's lovely."

"So is the girl," he told her, smiling.

"Where's Denise?" Chester asked.

Dan gave him a sardonic look. "Waiting to make an effective entrance after the audience has assembled, if I know my fair cousin."

Apparently he did, for the front door was flung open and Denise stood for a moment framed in the brightly lighted entrance, looking out at them. She wore a gold sheath gown, gold slippers, and there was a gold jeweled pin in her hair, which was piled high on her head in soft gold curls.

Then she came forward, holding out both hands in a pretty but calculated gesture of greeting. "Am I late?" she asked.

Chester looked down adoringly into the big blue eyes. He gulped. "Just in time. Just right."

145

Denise's eyes flickered to Jill's white dress. She smiled brilliantly. "How wise you are to wear those simple styles, Gillian. They suit you."

Dan grinned. "It's your turn to shoot," he told Jill. "Open season. Or do you hold your fire?"

Jill held her temper under control. For some reason Denise Clayton was determined to treat her with deliberate discourtesy. Some answers crowded to Jill's lips and she forced them back. Rudeness, her father had told her long ago, reflected only on the person who was guilty of it, never on his or her victim.

"I can think of only one thing at a time," she said lightly. "Right now I am thinking about food."

"At least it's an easy wish to gratify." Dan helped her into the front seat of his convertible. It seemed natural that Denise and Chester should be paired off and get in the back of the car.

The tables at the inn were already filled except for one on the edge of the dance floor. The waiter whipped off the RESERVED sign. A small but excellent orchestra was playing softly.

"I hope," Denise said in a discontented voice—she had not forgiven her cousin for relegating her to the back seat, though she had practically asked herself to the dinner dance—"the food is better here than it used to be."

"It's out of this world," Jill assured her. "I can fervently recommend the crabmeat in those little patty shells with—"

Dan's eyes glinted with amusement while she promptly gave her order. "You look like an illustration for something lovely and elusive and then you display this unseemly, not to say gross, appetite for food. Let's dance while they decide what they are going to order."

He danced smoothly and easily, watching with smiling eyes while Jill exchanged gay words with most of the young couples. What a simple friendly girl she was! She saw his expression.

"You're laughing at me," she accused him.

"I'm smiling with delight. I've never seen anyone who enjoys living as much as you do."

"But how can anyone help it?" she demanded.

Following Dan's skillful lead she circled the room. They passed their table, where, to her surprise, Denise and Chester still sat. They were deep in conversation, their heads close together. Dan took a quick look at Jill, but the radiance had not faded from her face.

"You mustn't worry about Denise," he said abruptly. "She's apt to have that effect on men at first. But it doesn't last. I know. I went through it myself and I've known others. But if my sweet cousin is poaching on your preserves, just leave her to me."

Jill laughed lightheartedly. "I'm not jealous."

"Aren't you?"

"Not a scrap," she said definitely. "I think you are laboring under a wrong impression. You believe that Chester and I are engaged. We aren't. We won't be. Ever. He's perfectly free to fall in love with any girl he chooses."

Dan brightened. There was an air of determination about him. "That means you are free, too. And here I've let two more important and endless days go by because I thought you were bespoke."

He pulled out her chair for her and they joined the other couple just as the first course was being served. The orchestra began a slow tango with a throbbing, irresistible rhythm. Denise, who had been watching the dancers with sulky eyes, put down her cocktail fork. Her lips parted in amazement.

Across the dance floor swept a striking

couple. Little by little, the other dancers drew back, watching them. They moved like professionals. They had, apparently, danced together so often that they moved as one person. In a moment the restaurant lights dimmed and a spotlight followed them, the graceful sinuous woman in black, her hair held in place by a high Spanish comb, long dramatic earrings; the man in white, the short dinner jacket molding broad, powerful shoulders.

"They're wonderful," Dan said. "What an exotic-looking woman."

"She looks like a gold-digger to me," Denise remarked spitefully. She laughed, her face bright with malice. "If she is, she's wasting her time."

"I doubt it," Dan answered. "He looks like quite a man to me, though he could double for that handsome chauffeur of yours."

"He is our chauffeur," Denise said sharply. "He is also a fortune hunter." She laughed again. "But he's got off on the wrong track again, unless I miss my bet."

The music stopped, leaving the couple beside their table. As a wave of applause swept over the room, Denise said, her voice clear and carrying, "Oh, Peters. I'll be ready to leave at twelve. Bring the car around then."

XIII

From the moment when Peter Carr had swept across the dance floor with the Spanish girl in his arms, Jill had been shaken as she had never been before. On top of the shock at watching the way Peter's eyes locked with Lola's as they danced—as though they had danced so often together!—had come Denise's revelations.

The Clayton chauffeur. A fortune hunter.

When Denise gave her imperious command Peter had flashed Jill one swift look and then murmured, "Of course, Miss Clayton," before he led his partner back to their table. The level gray eyes that had warmed with laughter and kindled with something else when he had looked at her were cold. The mouth which had had such tenderness and compassion had been hard. The face had been bleak, remote, the face of a stranger.

It was apparent that Lola Thompkins had

not known of Peter Carr's present occupation, however well she might—must—have known him in the past. She was furious. Her anger and humiliation were amply revealed by her gestures, by her expression, by the flood of words which they could see but could not hear.

Peter Carr called for his check and the couple left abruptly. But though they passed close to the table where Jill was sitting, Peter did not again look in her direction.

She tried to pretend that she was enjoying herself, but she could not swallow the dinner she had ordered so enthusiastically; she felt too tired to drag herself around the dance floor; it was impossible to maintain a gay smile on her lips.

Chester, with whom she was dancing, looked down at her in concern.

"What's wrong, Jill? You look so terribly white."

"A headache," she said. "A violent headache."

"I've begged you over and over to go away. You aren't well, Jill. At least, I'm glad you are willing to admit it."

"You don't look so well yourself," Jill retorted.

Chester's face was drawn and white, his

eyes were red-rimmed.

"No sleep. Guess I'm getting to be an old man. Ever hear how George Washington went to consult a doctor about his 'approaching decay' when he was only twenty-seven?"

"Chester, you were really splendid last night. You saved Peter Carr's life."

"How do you know?" The remark was so explosive that she stared at him in amazement.

"You needn't bite my head off," she said.

"Sorry. Only let's forget last night. Shall we?"

Thinking of the moment when she had been in Peter Carr's arms the night before, of the moment when she had heard his passionate words, Jill nodded. "We'll forget it," she agreed wearily.

They had reached their table by now. "I'll take you home," Chester offered, a shade reluctantly, after he had explained about Jill's headache.

"Nonsense, I'll drive her back," Dan said promptly. "You and Denise —" and he grinned—"will have the Clayton car, you know. Come on, little one," he said gently. "I'll see you get home safely."

He put her wrap over her shoulders and opened the top of the convertible. "Put your head against the back of the seat and rest. It was hot in there. A little cool air will do you good."

He drove slowly, aimlessly, following winding tree-lined lanes. The night was so still that she could hear the gentle rustling of the leaves. Then he took the river road. The sky was studded with stars.

Night let her sable curtain down
And pinned it with a star.

Jill quoted the lines softly and was silent again. Beside her Dan Holt made no attempt to break into her thoughts. Now and then, he stole a quick look at the shadowy figure beside him, but he remained quiet and she was grateful to him. Then, as the moonlight touched her arm and he could make out the faint line of the burn, he spoke.

"Does that burn hurt you much?"

"Not really." She added in explanation, "I went to the fire last night."

"You did! I didn't see you there. But — you must have got dangerously close —"

"I didn't," Jill said clearly. "Someone knocked me out and dragged me against the end of the building that collapsed."

Dan caught his breath sharply. He doesn't

believe me, Jill thought in despair. No one believes me. The Bennetts talk about my imagination, my nerves. And now this supposed headache—

After a moment he said, "But—if that happened—how did you escape with only one burn on your arm?"

"Peter Carr—the Clayton chauffeur—found me and got me away."

"He's the one who was trapped in the building, isn't he? Unusual man for a chauffeur. His manner and bearing. Very unusual. I noticed tonight that he seems to patronize the same English tailor I do. And that girl with him—"

"She was very attractive," Jill said slowly.

"You can say that again! All the glamor of Hollywood and as exciting as a time fuse. I wonder where Carr ever found her? I'll say for the Clayton chauffeur he has terrific taste in women. I'd hate to have him for serious competition, chauffeur or no chauffeur. He's got something any woman could fall for."

He was silent a moment, pondering. "You know, that sweet cousin of mine is going to run head on into trouble if she ever pulls a trick like that again. She didn't need the car. She was deliberately embarrassing him, baiting him, humiliating him in front of that most attractive woman."

"Denise said he was a fortune hunter," Jill said dully.

"So she did." After a moment's thought Dan commented, "Look here, Jill, do you think there's any chance Carr was the one who knocked you out and then 'saved' you? The Bellamy—"

"The Bellamy heiress," she said dryly. "Yes, I know. Dan, my head's worse. Will you please take me home?"

It was only ten o'clock when Jill said good night to Dan Holt at the door of the Bennett house. He held her hand tightly.

"I'm sorry I spoiled your evening," she said contritely. "You needn't have come with me."

Jill stole quietly up to her room, put the gardenia in a wide flat bowl, removed the white evening dress, and slipped into a blue velvet housecoat with matching slippers. She switched off the light and stretched out on a chaise longue, looking across the lawn at the Clayton swimming pool, which reflected the moon.

The night was perfect, the moon sailed serenely through clear skies. The room was scented by the gardenia, its petals as white as the moonlight. She switched on the small radio beside her, turning the volume low. A man's tenor voice sang:

O moon of my delight that know'st no wane
The moon of heaven is rising once again.

The majestic beauty of the night, the delicate beauty of the flower, the tender beauty of the man's voice were more than she could bear. Jill buried her head in a tiny satin pillow and her body was racked with sobs. It was not her head that ached, it was her heart.

The paroxysm was as brief as it was violent. She pushed the sodden pillow away from her and dried her eyes. A slim hand reached out to silence the radio, to stop the poignant music. Because she was by nature sunny-hearted, she was surprised at her own outburst, her own despairing grief. What had happened to her?

Fortune hunter. Somehow, that was the intolerable thing. Can my heart be so wrong, she thought. *Follow your heart,* her father had advised her. She remembered how he had always trusted her judgment of people. On one occasion, he had even decided not to buy a Manet because Jill had not liked the dealer. Later, when the canvas was proved to spurious, he had come proudly to tell her.

"How do you do it?" he had demanded.

"His eyes were too wide and honest," Jill had explained. "He tried too hard to look trustworthy."

"I believe you are really a witch in disguise," her father had teased her. "But just the same, I wish I had your instinctive wisdom about people."

She had met Peter Carr and fallen in love with him at once. Twice he had saved her, once when she was locked in the warehouse with the rats, once when she had been knocked out and left to die at the fire. She had heard his voice when consciousness returned, heard his words. He loved her. He must love her.

She understood now why he had never called her, never come to see her. As the Claytons' chauffeur that would have been impossible for him. But why was he a chauffeur, this man with his obvious breeding and education? And why, above all, the Claytons' chauffeur? Because of Denise? Then who was Lola Thompkins, whom he had pretended not to know? Whom he obviously knew very well. What was she doing in Mapleville? He had been taken aback when she had appeared at Mrs. Meam's house.

Jill got up and paced the floor, the long robe swirling around her feet, the velvet slippers noiseless in the quiet night. Denise knew about Peter Carr. She could ask her about him. After his appearance at the inn, the best-dressed, most distinguished-looking man there, her curiosity would be natural enough.

No, she thought, not Denise. I can't. That girl poisons everything she touches. I don't want to hear her speak of Peter. Anyhow, she's as sharp as a needle. She might guess how I feel about him. No, not Denise.

Car lights brightened the room for a moment, turned in at the Clayton driveway. There were voices, the door slammed, the car rolled smoothly into the garage and the lights went out.

Then Denise laughed under Jill's window. She and Chester were standing side by side on the lawn.

"He must be a quick-change artist or an actor," Chester was saying.

"Who?"

"Your chauffeur. First he appeared in dinner clothes, looking like an advertisement for What the Well-Dressed Man Will Wear, and then in chauffeur's uniform, looking like a graven image."

"He didn't like having his evening broken up and his date spoiled." Denise sounded amused.

"You can hardly blame him for that. The striking-looking girl with him was furious. I think she was giving him a bad time."

"I noticed," Denise said demurely. "That was his mistake. He shouldn't have risked taking her to a place frequented by his employers. There are roadhouses that would have been more suitable to his position."

"You know," Chester said, "he didn't strike me as being out of place at the inn. There's a quality about him—he appeared more like the guest of honor."

"That," Denise said tartly, "is part of his stock in trade."

"What do you mean?"

"What I said at dinner. He's a born crook. A fortune hunter. Four years ago, he tried every way he could think of to make me marry him so he could get his hands on my money. I got rid of him then, but now he's back as Dad's chauffeur."

"Why?"

"I wish I knew," Denise admitted. "He's up to something. He can't fool me about that. All Dad told me was that he'd hired him as a chauffeur for the summer and that we were to call him Peter Carr."

"Oh, then that's not his real name?"

"Oh no, of course not. He's — " Denise broke off with a gasp. "Jeepers! I promised Dad not to tell anyone and I almost did. There's something about you, Chester. I find myself talking my head off and usually I'm awfully reserved with strangers."

"I'm not a stranger."

"I felt that right away," Denise said softly. She laid a small hand on his arm, looked up at him. "You're so different from men like — Peters. You're so strong and dependable. He's so weak."

"In all justice," Chester said honestly, "I'll have to admit there was nothing weak about him last night at the fire. He was trapped in the warehouse. When I got a ladder up there he swung out like a cat and caught it."

"Trapped in the warehouse," Denise said thoughtfully. "I wonder what he was doing in there."

"Fighting the fire, of course."

"From inside a burning building? It's more likely that he set it. Anyhow, why are we talking about him when you are here?" Denise moved back a step to look up into his face.

"Don't look at me like that, Denise,"

Chester begged her. "Don't torment me so."

"Torment you?" she said in mock surprise, provocation in her manner.

"You know you do. You know exactly how much power you have over me."

"And don't you like being tormented?"

"Denise! You know darned well how I feel. If only I were free—"

There was a little pause. Denise said coolly, "Gillian Bellamy, of course."

"Why—of course?" There was sudden tension in Chester's voice. He sounded startled.

Denise laughed. "With her money? What else could you do? I heard your mother warning Dan off the premises, putting up a sign: 'Private property.'" She added quietly, "Don't misunderstand me, Chester. I'm not blaming you. With a fortune like that in reach you'd be a fool not at least to make a try for it."

"Denise," he said desperately, "you don't really understand at all."

She stood on tiptoe, brushed his cheek with a light kiss. "There," she said laughing, "you'll have something pleasant to remember."

She ran across the lawn to her house, the gold dress glittering in the moonlight.

Chester stood looking after her. Jill heard him make a queer sound, almost like a strangled sob, and then he went quickly to the side door. In a few moments she heard lagging footsteps as he climbed the stairs to his room. A door closed softly.

Only then did it occur to Jill that she had unintentionally been eavesdropping on a conversation which she had no right to hear.

For a long time she continued to sit at the dark window, her thoughts more depressed than they had ever been in her life. At length she took a long breath and released it in a sigh. She started to get up from the chaise lounge when an oblong of yellow light appeared in the night. It was a window in the apartment over the Claytons' garage.

A light hung over a small table near the window. She saw it reflected on Peter's head, bent intently over something he held in his hand. He lifted it and the light fell more clearly on the object. A revolver! He stood up and dropped it in his pocket. A moment later the light went out.

Jill leaned forward breathlessly, her heart thudding. What did it mean? Why was he armed? Then she saw a shadow dart around the corner of the garage. Where was he going? What on earth was he planning to do?

XIV

Earlier that evening, Jim Trevor had sat on the porch swing at Mrs. Meam's house waiting for Lola Thompkins. The night was gloriously warm and still. There was no sound but the rustling of leaves that sounded like soft rain. The scent of roses filled the air. The sky was sprinkled with stars.

Jim took a long breath. For the first time since his return to Mapleville he had a sense of homecoming. So far he had not gone near the house his father still owned. There wasn't the market there used to be for big places like that, and not enough domestic help available. It would probably prove to be a white elephant. Still, he had been relieved when Andrew Trevor had decided to put it on the market. After all, no Trevor would ever again live in Mapleville.

But now he wasn't so sure. If he could

spend his summers in this New England village, with its roots deep in the rich history of the American past, it would balance the winters in New York, with their stimulus and excitement and high-speed living. That could be a good life, he thought. And suppose—a man could dream, couldn't he?—he had a wife like Gillian Bellamy at his side, radiant, lovely, courageous.

He took a firm grasp on his runaway imagination. This wouldn't do. He had to keep his feet on the ground, remember the facts. He couldn't even approach Jill as himself, only as the Clayton chauffeur. And, anyhow, Jill was engaged to marry Chester Bennett. Would she ever realize that she didn't really love him?

There was a click of high heels on the stairs, the scent of heavy perfume, and Lola opened the screen door, came out on the porch, both hands outstretched.

"Jim, darling! Have you been waiting long?"

"It didn't seem long," he answered truthfully and then realized that he had made a mistake. Lola had misunderstood him.

Her face lighted up. "You mean it? Really? But then what made you so hard to get? I practically forced you to ask me tonight."

He took the exquisite Spanish shawl out of her hands and put it over her shoulders. "You look very much the señorita," he said, smiling.

"Only half of me," she replied. "My mother was Spanish but my father was all Yankee trader."

And how, Jim thought in amusement. He said aloud, "Where's that car you rented?"

She handed him the key. "It's the Ford parked in front. I thought I might as well see some of the country while I'm here."

He closed the door behind him, started the car. As he drove toward the inn he asked quietly, "What are you doing here, Lola?"

She looked at the man beside her, at the fine profile, the good forehead, the strong jaw, the firm and sensitive mouth, the perfectly cut dinner clothes, the air of unstressed power that had always impressed her.

"I came for you," she said in her husky voice. "You nearly loved me once, Jim. I believe in fighting for what I want. You haven't married. You aren't engaged. I thought I'd remind you that Lola Thompkins is still around, waiting for you to make up your mind."

"Lola!"

There was embarrassment in his voice but

there was also distaste. There was no pleasant way in which a man could tell a woman that he did not love her, that he did not want her love. His mistake had been in spending so much time with her when he had been visiting his father.

There were no words exchanged between them on the short drive to the inn. Jim wondered awkwardly how he could handle the situation Lola had forced upon him without hurting her too much, and leaving her pride intact. Lola seemed content to wait. A quick look showed the faint smile playing around her mouth.

Jim handed the car key to the attendant outside the inn and Lola preceded him to the table he had reserved. They were early and only half the tables were occupied. When they had ordered, she turned to him.

"Jim," she began.

"Peter Carr," he reminded her quietly.

"But why? I can't understand it. A man like you hiding behind a strange name."

"I can't explain. All I can tell you is that I am doing a confidential job and this seemed the best way to handle it."

"You're not in the FBI or anything, are you?"

Jim laughed outright. "Good lord, no! I'm

still with the law firm."

"But that's another thing I can't understand. Why must you shackle yourself with a job? You don't have to work."

"I started in law school virtually penniless except for my tuition. I have learned the hard way that money—plenty of it—can vanish overnight. Anyhow, I believe in the value and importance of the law and I'd like to make a real place for myself in it, a real contribution. It's a noble profession, Lola, in spite of the shysters and the people who use it for their own corrupt purposes. And I'm damned if I am willing to be a playboy, doing nothing worthwhile at all."

Lola leaned toward him and he was aware of the low-cut dress, of her gleaming shoulders, of the overpowering perfume she wore.

"You aren't going to explain what you are really doing here?"

"I can't. You must accept that, Lola. And forget it."

There was a sulky twist to her full mouth. Then she laughed. "All right, we'll forget it. If you are the kind of man who likes to appear mysterious it's all right with me."

Little by little, the room filled, and suddenly Jim saw Jill on the dance floor, moving lightly in the arms of Dan Holt, who was laughing with her. Jill's gay ripple of laughter rang out for a moment. Jim scowled. What did that guy have that could amuse her so much?

He started as a hand covered his own and long nails bit unexpectedly into his flesh.

"Jim!"

"Sorry," he said.

"I've spoken to you three times," Lola said, storm signals in her eyes. "When a man takes me out for the evening I expect at least that he'll remember I'm there."

"Forgive me, Lola."

"She's the one, isn't she?" Lola said quietly.

Jim's eyes automatically went to Jill, who was returning to her table.

"The girl with the gold hair and the gold dress. The one you used to call your golden girl."

"Yes, she's the golden girl. But not mine."

"Who is she?"

"Denise Clayton."

"So that's why you are here." Lola crumbled a roll in nervous fingers.

"No," Jim said deliberately, "Denise has nothing to do with my being here."

"I don't believe you," she said sullenly.

The dance band began the slow irresistible tango. Jim held out his hand. "Come on," he said persuasively. She brightened and got up promptly.

After the debacle at the inn—Denise's rudeness, Lola's tantrum—Jim returned to his room above the garage, his emotions a seething turmoil. He could not sleep. After all, he had come here to guard Jill. Action was what he needed. He would do a little scouting and get to the bottom of this warehouse fire and arson business.

He stole across the lawn. Beautiful as the moonlight was, he regretted it now. He moved noiselessly from the protection of one tree to another, careful to expose himself as little as possible. He reached the dark bulk of the Bennett garage, a long affair with a big toolroom and stalls for three cars. Probably it would be locked. There was a gravel driveway. Approaching the building from the front would be a noisy business. Better try a side window.

Cr-unch! Cr-unch!

He drew back, pressing himself against the wall. His clothes were dark but his face might be seen in the moonlight. Someone was on the gravel driveway.

"A fool place to meet," a man grunted.

Carefully Jim edged his way around the corner of the garage. An airplane went overhead, the motors so loud he missed the next words.

". . . burned up, completely destroyed," the second man said.

The first man's voice was louder. "I get my money just the same."

"Quiet! Not so loud."

The voice dropped to an indistinguishable rumble. Jim strained to hear.

"Suppose I told," the first man began, and at his companion's horrified exclamation he chuckled softly.

"You wouldn't do that!"

"Wouldn't I?"

"You wouldn't dare."

"What do I have to lose? But you—"

Jim crept as close to the garage door as he could get without attracting attention.

". . . can't pay you."

"You'll have to work out something. I don't intend to go on hiding like this."

Hiding! John Jones! Jim was sure of it. He took an incautious step forward, his shoe grated on gravel. Stopped. There wasn't a sound. He held his breath. Had he scared them off? They weren't speaking.

Unexpectedly, something struck him between the shoulders, throwing him off balance. The man behind him rushed him at a stumbling run across the lawn to the edge of the Clayton swimming pool. A hand thrust hard and he plunged into the water.

He bobbed up almost immediately. Running feet thudded across the lawn. Jim hauled himself out of the pool and stood dripping on the lawn.

This was the strangest part of the whole business. The man who had rushed him into the pool was bigger, stronger than he. But he hadn't wanted to hurt him. He had simply wanted to get away unseen.

There was no chance of catching him now. Jim went slowly back to his room, water dripping from his clothes. He had learned a lot tonight. More than one man was involved in the attacks on Jill. The one in hiding must be John Jones. But the one who refused to pay —who was he? And why had he lied about the boxes, pretended they had been destroyed in the fire?

Or didn't he know? Was there still a third man involved?

XV

Jill shook her head at her reflection in the mirror. There were dark circles under her eyes and a droop to the corners of her mouth. That's what a sleepless night had done to her. She had tossed restlessly until daybreak.

Why had Peter Carr been armed and where had he gone in the night? What did he plan to do that would require using a revolver?

For hours the same questions had hammered at her mind. Who was the man who called himself Peter Carr, whose watch bore the initials J.T.? What was he doing here? He had tried in every possible way to marry Denise Clayton and get his hands on her money. Denise thought he might have set fire to the warehouse. Dan Holt thought he had pretended to "save" her because she was the Bellamy heiress. Had Peter been in the warehouse for some reason the day she was locked in? He had never explained how he happened to be near a deserted building on a dead-end road.

And there was Aunt Sally's lodger, the glamorous Lola Thompkins, whom Peter had seemed not to know, whom he obviously knew so well.

Jill looked clear-eyed at the mass of evidence that weighed against Peter Carr. Then she listened to her heart. I don't believe it, she told herself firmly. I believe in Peter.

She glanced again at the face which reflected her sleepless night and shook her head disapprovingly. Never lose your trust, blind trust, she told herself. Follow your heart.

She slipped into a white bathing suit, put on sandals, caught up her cap and went softly downstairs, trying not to arouse the sleeping household.

The lawn sparkled with dew and a tiny rabbit hopped off in haste as she appeared. The trees looked freshly washed in their green finery, the leaves sparkling as though prepared for the special festival of a new day.

She ran across the cool grass to the pool and sat on the edge to test the water. Br-r-r. It had not warmed up after the cool New England night. For a moment she hesitated, shivering. Then she pulled on her cap and climbed swiftly up to the diving board. For a moment she poised on the edge, bouncing lightly up and down. Then, with arms wide-spread, she made a perfect swan dive.

She cut cleanly through the water and came up, swimming vigorously toward the end of the pool. The water had been like ice. Her breath was cut off with the shock. She turned, kicked backward, and swam to the other end. Up and back, up and back, with long strong easy strokes until the water no longer felt cold. She turned on her back to float, eyes closed, and felt the sun warm on her face.

I'm happy, she thought suddenly. This is a perfect moment. I'll remember it always. But why? What gives me this sudden all-pervasive joy? She did not need to ask herself the question because she knew the answer. She had conquered her fears and her doubts and she was left with the firm support of her blind, liberating trust.

She turned on her face, eyes open under the water. There was some object on the bottom of the pool. A rock. Surely the Clayton gardener, who checked the pool every day, would not have been so careless. She dived down and groped for it, came up to fill her lungs with air. Down again. It was the bowl of a pipe. She went down several times before she found the stem, the oddly curved stem, which had been broken off.

For a long time she sat on the edge of the pool staring thoughtfully at Peter Carr's broken pipe. He would never have left it there if he had been aware of his loss. Then what had happened? Where had he gone in the night with that revolver? How had his pipe been broken and dropped in the pool? Peter — could he have been hurt? She shivered with the sudden cold that was in her heart.

She looked up at the window of Peter's room over the Clayton garage. For a moment she was almost unbearably tempted to go up, to see whether he was all right.

Somewhere in the distance a truck backfired. The village was beginning to wake up. Someone came out of the side door of the Clayton house. It was Dan Holt, wearing swimming trunks. He caught sight of her and his face lighted up. He waved.

Jill waved back, looked at the broken pieces of the pipe. For some reason she did not want to tell Dan about them. But where could she hide them? Her bathing suit fitted like a glove. She ripped off her cap, dropped the two pieces of the pipe into it. She shook her hair loose so that the damp curls at the end could dry in the sun.

"Hi, there," Dan said. "Headache gone?"

"Not a trace."

"You look like a mermaid." His face fell as he saw her fold up her bathing cap. "Are you going in already?"

"I've been here quite a while and I'm beginning to get chilled."

He hid his disappointment. "Then I won't keep you. Better have a hot shower."

She nodded and ran back across the lawn to the house. She slipped in by the side door, which she had left unlocked, and started quickly up the back stairs. From the kitchen, where breakfast was being prepared, came the quiet voices of the two maids and the subdued sound of dishes and glassware.

As she reached the second floor, the quiet was shattered. Raised voices were coming from Chester's room.

"My own son!" Bennett was shouting. "My own son!"

The door of the Bennetts' bedroom was ajar and Jill could see something move in the opening, the dreary mustard-colored dressing gown Mrs. Bennett had recently bought. Noiselessly Jill crept up to her own door and opened it.

"I've hoped against hope," Bennett went on, his voice shaking, "that I was mistaken. I didn't want to believe you were capable—"

For the first time Chester spoke. His tone was so unlike his usual good-humored voice that at first Jill failed to recognize it.

"Not so loud," he advised his father. "You can be heard over at the Claytons'."

"I don't give a—"

"You'll wake Jill. Do you want her to hear all this?"

"Oh, God," his father said, in a kind of groan. "Not Gillian. I won't have her dragged into this."

Chester's laugh was like a blow across the face.

Jill closed her door softly, turned on her shower and stripped off the wet bathing suit. Under the shower, to her relief, she could hear no sound but the running water. She toweled briskly until her skin glowed and then dressed in a deep blue cotton dress with a round white collar of crisp organdy.

She rubbed her hair dry, brushed it until it shone. The eyes of the girl in the mirror were wide and startled. She had been right in suspecting that Mr. Bennett was worried about Chester, that there was tension of some kind between father and son. What she had not been prepared for was the savage hostility, the naked anger in both voices. Something was terribly wrong in the Bennett house.

The voices seemed to have lost their fury now. The men were talking in lowered tones. Then, unexpectedly, Mr. Bennett's voice rose in a frenzied cry.

"No! No, by God, you can't do that! I'll stop you. I'll stop—"

"Dad!" Chester cried out in alarm.

There was a heavy crash from Chester's room. "Dad!" he cried again. "Have you hurt yourself? Are you all right? Dad, say something."

Someone ran down the hall, flung open the door of Chester's room.

"William!" Mrs. Bennett screamed. "William, what's happened to you? Chester, help me get him on the bed."

Jill hesitated, her hand on the doorknob, in an agony of indecision. Should she help? Would they prefer to have her pretend that she had not overheard the quarrel? Though everyone in the house must have heard it by now.

"I'll do it, Mother," Chester said. "I can manage alone. He's just fainted, I think."

There were movements, the creak of a bed as Mr. Bennett was lifted onto it.

"He looks so terribly white," Mrs. Bennett choked. "It's his heart. He can't stand physical or emotional strain. You should have known better than to let him excite himself."

Chester gave a sharp bark of bitter laughter. "I didn't start this, Mother. I've been trying to sidestep it for weeks."

"But you must have done something to upset him. You know how your father loves you. He'd never be angry like that unless you did something very wrong. He was just beside himself."

"I tell you I didn't start this, Mother."

"Well, the harm's done now. No use arguing about it. Oh, don't just stand there. Get me that heart medicine, quick, and some water."

Jill went into the hallway, saw the open door of Chester's room. Mr. Bennett, a dressing gown over his pajamas, lay on the bed, his face colorless except for the ominously blue lips, his eyes closed, his mouth slack. Mrs. Bennett, pin-curled hair in a net, the mustard robe flung over her nightgown, was bending over him.

Chester, dressed except for a necktie, was standing at the foot of the bed, breathing quickly from the exertion of lifting his heavy father, a queer expression on his face as he looked down at the unconscious man. It was a look oddly like despair.

"Quick," Mrs. Bennett repeated.

"Can I help?" Jill asked from the doorway.

"Get the doctor right away, Gillian," Mrs. Bennett instructed her. "Tell him that William has had a serious heart attack and he is still unconscious. And I must say, Gillian, if he hadn't strained himself at the fire, fighting for your property, this would never have happened."

Jill ran down the stairs to dial the doctor's number. She was stung by the older woman's unjust comment. It wasn't fair to blame her for her guardian's heart attack. Then she forced herself to remember Mrs. Bennett's past kindnesses, to remember that she was terribly upset and worried. She hadn't really meant it.

A quiet voice answered the telephone and she poured out her story breathlessly.

"You are lucky, Miss Bellamy," the doctor told her, his slow voice steadying her panic. "I was just leaving for the hospital. I'll be there within ten minutes."

He was as good as his word. At the insistence of the excited maids, Jill ate her breakfast while she waited for the doctor's report.

He came into the breakfast room as she

was finishing. A stoop-shouldered man with a lined face and eyes that looked as though he never had enough sleep.

"Dr. Wall! How is he?"

"Do you think there is any more coffee in that pot?" he asked.

While he drank coffee and ate a hot muffin lavishly spread with butter, he explained the situation.

"He is overweight. He eats too much and drinks too much and smokes too much. He gets no regular exercise and then every so often he overexerts. His heart is in poor shape. I've been warning him for months. But he's stubborn. Maybe this is the best thing that could happen. It may shock him into taking care of himself. At least it will make him take it easy for a while. I wanted to put him in the hospital but he won't hear of it. Anyhow," the doctor added with a weary sigh, "we never have enough hospital beds for our acute cases, let alone the chronic ones."

He set down the coffee cup. "Well, I'll keep him in bed for a week and I warned Maud not to let him go off his diet."

Unexpectedly he asked, his keen eyes on her face, "What set off the trouble this morning?"

"He and Chester had a quarrel," Jill

explained reluctantly.

"Thought so. Maud is in a dither and Chester looks like death. Wonder what set those two at odds. I always thought that was a singularly close father and son relationship. Except, of course, that Chester refused to go into his father's business."

"It must have been a disappointment," Jill said. "Mr. Bennett was speaking of it just recently. He seems to have felt badly about it."

Dr. Wall looked at his watch and grunted. "Off to a late start, as usual. Be nice if each day had thirty-six hours. I might catch up someday."

He had barely gone when Chester came downstairs.

"How is your father?" Jill asked.

Chester's face wore a queer, set look. "He's conscious. The doctor says he'll be all right, but he is going to have to stay in bed for a few days. Did the doctor say anything more to you?"

It seemed to her that he was watching her in a strange, distrustful way.

"Just —" Jill hesitated and then went on in a rush — "that he doesn't want your father upset again."

"Upset." Chester's lips twisted in a grimace.

"He's going to be lot more upset than that before we get through, or I'll be very much surprised."

"Chester." Jill caught his sleeve, looked pleadingly into his haggard face. "Chester, don't forget—he's your father."

He turned on his heel and went out without a word.

XVI

Jill got out her little car and drove to the nearest filling station.

"Fill 'er up?" the attendant asked.

She laughed. "I practically pushed it all the way here. With the gauge marked empty I must have made the whole trip on air or hope or something."

"Empty! With the mileage you get on this little foreign job? Why, I filled that tank day before yesterday. You must have been going places."

"Will you check the oil?" Jill asked to avoid any comment.

"I checked the oil, water, battery, and the air in the tires last time. The Bennetts sure keep that car in good condition for you."

Except when the brakes fail to work, Jill thought.

So it was true that gasoline had been

siphoned out of her car. She found herself shivering, though the sun was hot on her head.

Mrs. Bennett had made clear that she would prefer to have her out of the way. It was obvious that she was blaming Jill for her husband's heart attack. She didn't want to admit to herself that the noisy and bitter quarrel between father and son had ever taken place. Chester could do no wrong. It was Jill who had caused the trouble because the warehouse belonged to her and William Bennett had become overtired fighting the fire.

Jill pulled the little car off the road and sat listening to summer, to the rustle of leaves, the drone of insects. The gentleness of that small green land smoothed the strain from her face like a caress. How lovely Connecticut was! Always in the distance the blue lines of hills, tree-shaded winding roads, green sunlit valleys.

I belong here, she thought. This is my country. My place. Here I want to put down my roots forever, to be a part of all this.

She started the car and drove on. Where the road branched she turned to the left because she caught a glint of blue water, a small still pool with ferns thick around it.

Beyond the pool was a stone fence with iron gates. The gates were closed and locked.

She got out of the car and climbed on the fence, looked down on the curving driveway that led to a long graystone house of gracious lines. The lawn and hedges were neglected, flowerbeds were choked with weeds. The blank windows stared back at her like blind eyes.

When at last Jill climbed off the stone fence she was stiff from sitting still but starry-eyed with excitement. In her imagination, which had caught fire, she had seen the windows filled with light, the lawn freshly mowed, the hedges trimmed, the flowerbeds a riot of color. She turned cautiously, almost afraid that her wishes had misled her.

The sign on the locked gate read: PENN MANOR — FOR SALE.

There was an acrid smell in her nostrils and Jill eased her foot on the brake pedal. This was what was left of the warehouse: charred timbers, burned ground, and the bitter smell of smoke. All that was left.

There was nothing — she leaned out of the open car window, staring — yes, something was moving. Then he straightened and she saw the man who was walking slowly, examining the burned area. Now and then, he stirred something with his foot. Now and then, he bent over for a closer inspection.

She turned off the motor and went swiftly to meet him.

"Good morning, Mr. Hartman. I see you are still continuing your investigation."

"Good morning, Miss Bellamy." He took her hand in a firm hand clasp. "You know, I owe you a real apology. I ought to be eating humble pie, right now. In fact, I am eating it and it chokes me."

Jill laughed. "Why all this attack of conscience?"

"Because I made a bad mistake about you," he told her gravely. "You see, I thought you were — well —"

"Go ahead," she encouraged him. "I can take it."

He looked at the vivid face with its direct eyes and firm warm mouth. "I guess you can at that. But you aren't going to like this and I can't say that I blame you."

"All you've done so far is to build up my curiosity to the bursting point."

"All right, you asked for it but don't blame me. I thought you were either — well, deliberately stringing me along with that story you

187

told me about the man John Jones or — or —"

"Well?"

"Or more than a little bit queer in the head," he admitted sheepishly.

Jill stared at him with incredulity. "Oh, really!" she exclaimed. She could feel her cheeks flaming. The man dared to tell her that he thought she was crazy.

"What made you think that?"

He gave her an odd look and hesitated. "Well, several things, actually," he said at length. "Anyhow, I've been in touch with the law firm that handles your legal matters. Garrison, Harper & Jennings. They are the ones who took out your insurance with us. I got hold of the head man himself, Mr. Garrison, and he gave me the lowdown. He said this man John Jones exists all right."

"Mr. Garrison!" Jill exclaimed in amazement. "But how does he know? What else did he tell you?"

"He said you had run into a lot of trouble up here and he suspected this fire was just part of the whole set-up."

"Mr. Garrison?" Jill threw out her hands in bewilderment. "I'm baffled, confounded and speechless. Who could have told him?"

"I don't know. But look here, Miss Bellamy. After talking to him, I would suggest that you had better be kind of careful. I don't like the sound of it."

"I'll be careful."

"Someone ought to be looking out for you." The insurance man smiled. "I wish I could hang around long enough to take on the job myself. First time I've ever thought it would be kind of nice to have a daughter."

"Thank you, kind sir," Jill laughed.

"Remember," he said, "you be real careful, young lady. And if you ever see that man Jones, you run screaming."

She laughed outright. "Famous last words. You make spiders creep up my spine. Ugh!"

He watched the lovely face with its telltale expression. "I hope you aren't holding out on me."

"I didn't mean to," she said contritely. "I wanted to tell you when you came to the house but—I could see you didn't really believe anything I said."

"I had a reason that seemed good to me though I suppose you wouldn't accept that. Can't blame you. Anyhow, I've apologized for my sins." He grinned. "Let's assume that I'll believe whatever you tell me. Fair enough?"

"Fair enough," Jill agreed.

"Shake on it?" He held out his hand and

she took it. "Now then, let's have the whole thing."

She told him about Peter Carr's story of the gasoline being poured on the warehouse floor, and he nodded as though it checked with his own findings. Later Peter had discovered the tank in her car was empty when it should have been filled.

At his request she told him how he could reach Peter Carr.

"You say he works for Roger Clayton? One of the governors of the Institute? One of the men who handle your estate?" The insurance man's voice was sharp. "You know what, Miss Bellamy, if you were my daughter I wouldn't be satisfied unless you had a good stout bodyguard."

"Heaven forbid! I'd feel like a gangster!" Jill waved to him and got in her car. A few minutes later, she parked outside the Institute. As a rule, few people visited it in the mornings, except for an occasional art student copying a painting. This morning the only cars in the parking lot were Roger Clayton's gleaming new Cadillac, Abraham Allen's shabby old Plymouth and, she saw in surprise, Chester's Chevrolet convertible. Chester never went near the Institute.

She stopped to speak to Joe Deakam,

who was sitting on a stone bench in the main room, working a crossword puzzle in his folded newspaper.

He looked up to ask, "What's a nine-letter word meaning stubborn?"

Jill counted on her fingers. "Obstinate."

"Hm. Wouldn't you think eight letters was enough for a little thing like being pig-headed?"

Jill laughed. "Are the governors busy?"

"They are in the director's room, except for Mr. Bennett. I understand he had a heart attack this morning."

Jill nodded. "He'll be all right, I think, if he takes care of himself."

"Glad to hear it. He's always nice and good-humored, no matter what comes up. Not much like old sour-faced Allen. Mr. Chester came down to take his father's place today and they are having a sort of meeting."

Jill's face fell. "Oh, then I'd be inter-rupting."

"Speaking for myself," Joe said gruffly, "you're always as welcome as the first flower-ing bush in spring. Anyways, the place be-longs to you. You've got a right here any time you want to come, if anyone has."

"I will have if I live to be twenty-one," she laughed. Her eyes widened. What had made her say that? Just because the insurance man had warned her to be careful. Fanciful. That's all it was. But she wished, somehow, the idea had not been so near the surface of her mind.

She opened the door of the director's room, a charming octagonal room. oak-paneled with a refectory table and four ancient carved armchairs. Because of the laxness of Thomas Bellamy's instructions, no one had ever been appointed director, but Abraham Allen, from the beginning, had taken the seat at the head of the table and appropriated to himself the privilege of acting as chairman of the meetings.

As Jill went in, Allen, who faced the door, said in a sharp tone, "I said we were not to be disturbed! Oh, it's you, Miss Bellamy."

He stood up ungraciously and Clayton and Chester followed suit. She saw then that they were checking a set of cards against long typewritten sheets of blue legal paper, which she recognized at once. This was the catalogue her father had made of his collection.

"If you haven't anything urgent in mind," Allen said, after giving her a limp hand-shake, "we're busy today."

"Sit down, my dear," Clayton said in his big voice, pulling out the fourth chair for her. "You'll be interested in this. Your father always said you knew almost as much about his collection as he did."

"Not quite." She smiled.

"Still, you studied the styles of the masters and he told me once that the head of one of the galleries told him you knew more about detecting fakes than anyone of your age he had ever met. With William away, we're just blundering along. None of us knows the first thing about this collection."

"The different ways of faking old masters fascinate me," Jill confessed. "Ever since I read about—"

Allen's thin lips tightened into a hard line. "Another time, we would doubtless appreciate Miss Bellamy's expert ideas, but just now we have a serious problem to face."

Jill felt as though he had slapped her. Obviously, Abraham Allen had no intention of taking seriously her training in art. Why, she thought furiously, he acts as though I don't even have a right to be here, a right to know what is happening to the Institute.

She turned to Chester, forced him to meet her eyes. "What's wrong?" she asked him bluntly.

Chester, his shaking hands rattling the pages he held, told her. "Some pages of your father's catalogue seem to be missing, Jill. There's no mention here of the Praxiteles bust."

"Damn it," Allen said angrily, "is there any reason for making that public at this time? Any loose talk could cause a scandal that would blow us all up."

"Gillian won't go in for loose talk," Roger Clayton said mildly.

She started to speak and saw the thoughtful way he was studying her.

"Any more accidents, Gillian, my dear?" he asked.

Her lips parted, closed again. Something in those watchful eyes warned her. Roger Clayton, like Hartman, suspected that she had willfully lied or — or —

She summoned up a gay smile. "All's well," she assured him. She wanted to join them, to check the catalogue with them, but she felt that she was an intruder here. Abraham Allen resented her presence. He resented her knowing the truth about the missing pages of the catalogue. If there had been any dereliction of duty on the part of the governors he did not intend to let her find it out.

"I won't keep you," she said. "I came because I need your approval to make a purchase."

"What kind of purchase?" Clayton asked, smiling. "A new dress? If you are like my daughter, you always think you have nothing to wear. And yet Denise has closets filled with clothes."

"Not a dress." Jill took a long breath. "A house. Penn Manor. It's for sale. I saw it this morning. I think I want it more than anything I ever saw in my life."

"But why?" Chester exploded suddenly. "What do you know about Penn Manor?"

"I want to live there," she explained eagerly. "Not now, of course. But when I am twenty-one. I'll need all that time to fix it up because it's been neglected, allowed to run down. I—oh, please, please—"

"This is ridiculous," Chester declared.

"That's for my governors to decide," she retorted. "You're not my governor. Your father is."

"I am representing my father here."

"Does he know it?" She was startled by his expression.

Clayton came around the table and led her gently to the door. "We'll think about it," he said genially. "Plenty of time. Plenty of time."

He patted her shoulder and closed the door behind her. In the quiet room with its walls hung with paintings, Jill paused to collect her temper. What right had Chester to interfere? What right had Abraham Allen to mock at her knowledge of art? What right had Roger Clayton to treat her like a child, a silly, frivolous child! She had been shut out of the meeting as though she were an intruder. And yet something was wrong with the Institute, something had gone wrong with her father's dream.

In the silence she heard Allen's voice from behind the closed door. It was shaking with fury. "Why did you have to tell her?"

XVII

Hartman took the chair that had been of-fered him, the only one in the small room, and from long practice summed up Peter Carr, Roger Clayton's chauffeur. Tall, slim, good-looking without being soft. Not soft at all. In fact, not a man he'd care to tangle with. But he had — well, *quality* was the best word the insurance man could think of. He moved with an air of assurance that was genuine, not mere compensation for a feel-ing of insecurity. He had a level-eyed direct-ness that built confidence. Not the usual chauffeur.

Peter Carr sat on the cot bed. "Well," he said in his pleasant voice, "what can I do for you?"

"Miss Bellamy gave me your name. She had an idea you could help me out. Give me a tip, maybe, about that warehouse fire."

197

The chauffeur looked from Hartman's business card to his face.

"What do you make of it?" His expression was unrevealing.

"Arson," Hartman said promptly. "That's what I told Mr. Bennett. He was really shook up. Takes his job seriously. And—" he paused for a moment—"that's what I told Mr. Garrison. You know who he is?"

The chauffeur nodded.

"Mr. Garrison thought it was just one of a series of things, part of the general picture." Hartman waited but the other man did not speak. "Personally, I think the Bellamy girl needs a bodyguard. This set-up is all wrong."

"I agree with you. And I can tell you this—the warehouse fire was set." The chauffeur described the removal of the boxes, the return of the unknown man, the smell of gasoline and then the fire that blazed up.

"And the gasoline had come from Miss Bellamy's car?"

"Well, it had come from somewhere and the tank was empty though the car had not been driven."

"What's this all about, Carr?" the insurance man said bluntly. "I've got enough information for my company—that is, if you are willing to testify. I suppose you are."

"I suppose I'd have to," the chauffeur said thoughtfully. "I hadn't thought of that. In this case, I'd better put you in the picture. My name is James Trevor, I'm in the law firm of Garrison, Harper & Jennings. They sent me up here, under cover, to find out just what was behind the series of attacks on Miss Bellamy."

"So that's it!" Hartman exclaimed. "You had me puzzled. Go on."

Jim told him the story succinctly.

"Well, that's quite a tale! Of course, it's all theory. Without those missing boxes you haven't a scrap of proof that they have anything to do with Miss Bellamy or the Institute."

"I'll find the proof," Jim said quietly.

The insurance man grinned. "Yeah. I guess you will at that. I know I'd put my money on you." He got up. "You've given me the help I need for my case. I'll be around these parts for several days. The Hartford office will be able to find me. If I can return the good deed, give me a call, will you?"

"I'll do that," Jim promised. "And thanks a lot. Playing a lone hand is not all it's cracked up to be."

"Brother, you're telling me!" the insurance man said fervently. "What's the next step?"

They left the garage together, walked toward the main section of the village. "That pick-up truck which was used to cart the stuff away. It's my only lead at the moment," Jim said. He had heard on the radio of the theft — and subsequent return — of a pick-up truck belonging to a local garage. The theft had taken place on the night of the warehouse fire.

"Good luck to you. I'll say you need it." Hartman turned for a parting shot. "And keep an eye on that beautiful girl. If anyone hurts her I believe I could strangle him with my bare hands."

"I know how you feel," Jim said quietly.

Hartman looked at him. "Oh," he said softly, "So it's like that, is it?"

"It's like that." Jim nodded and walked swiftly away.

The garage which had been mentioned in the newscast as owner of the stolen pick-up truck was only a few blocks from the Green.

The garage man straightened up and pushed back his cap. "Well, judging by the mileage that shows and the number of miles the car gets per gallon — it's hardly been driven at all. Wait a sec, chief, until I look up the last mileage reading. We keep track of it on cars and trucks we rent out."

Jim waited patiently. That morning, it had occurred to him that if he could find out how far the stolen pick-up truck had been driven he would be in a better position to track down the missing boxes.

"Well, I'll be darned. Only three miles. That's queer." The truck owner gave Jim a puzzled look. "Why would anyone take the risk of stealing it just for a little jaunt like that? A little over a mile each way?"

"Probably he had to move some stuff in a hurry."

"And he wasn't willing to pay what I charge by the hour? What a cheapskate!"

"It might have been stolen goods," Jim pointed out.

The garage man gave him a swift look. "Yeah," he said slowly. "You didn't say why you were interested, mister."

Jim slipped a five-dollar bill into his hand. "I'm the curious type," he said lightly, and strolled off.

Once out of sight of the garage he did some quick figuring. Then he took a large-scale map of Mapleville and vicinity out of his pocket and drew a circle with the warehouse as the center.

It was a nice day for a walk and Clayton

had told him he'd be free to use the time as he liked. From what he remembered of Mapleville, he could eliminate almost all the buildings contained within the circumference of his circle. These were mostly working dairy farms. There would be dogs to give warning of the arrival of any stranger. Boxes could not be hidden without the risk of almost immediate discovery.

What then? There were only four possibilities. Jim walked swiftly, head back, aware of the lush beauty of midsummer. The first possibility he remembered was an abandoned farm. When he reached it, he saw the trucks and workmen's cars lining the road. An excavation was being dug. The old building had been torn down to make room for what was apparently going to be a huge house. No point in lingering here.

At the second, he did not even check his stride. This farm had been converted into a summer camp for small boys. Only a madman would risk concealing boxes here.

That left two possibilities: the house belonging to Abraham Allen and Penn Manor, his father's former home.

Allen! Jim's lips tightened. From the day when he had returned to Mapleville, he had known that sooner or later he must have a showdown with Allen. In one way or another, he intended to force him to clear Andrew Trevor's name, if he had to shake the truth out of him.

It was queer that Abraham Allen should be involved not only with his father but with Gillian Bellamy's father. If he was the man who had removed the boxes, Jim intended to expose him in a way that would end his political ambitions forever.

Abraham Allen lived in a converted farmhouse which had been modernized and expanded. Having been rebuilt without taste, it was a curious hodgepodge of New England farmhouse plus a long modern wing that seemed to have been tacked on. The garage doors were open and the car was gone. There were no signs of life. Allen employed an elderly housekeeper and her son as his whole domestic staff.

Jim leaned against a post and looked over the property. The lawn was as smooth as a billiard table, a considerable feat in Connecticut soil with its boulders which continually work to the surface. There were no flowerbeds, no place where the ground had been turned up.

Jim looked up at the windows. Nothing moved behind them. He slipped into the grounds and crossed the lawn. From the side, he could see the back of the property. There was an unexpectedly large vegetable garden and a man in overalls was bending down, working between the neat rows. Allen would never have buried the boxes where his gardener might unearth them.

Remembering Allen's slight build and his age, it seemed unlikely to Jim that he could have carried the boxes up to the attic. That left the basement or the toolroom of the garage. He examined the toolroom in one hasty look. It was as neat and as well organized as the shelves of a hardware store. That left the basement.

He waited inside the garage until he saw the gardener stoop again, back turned to him. Then he ran across the driveway and stood listening at the screen door of the kitchen. There was no one in the kitchen. He let himself in softly and looked for the cellar door. Upstairs he heard heavy steps, the elderly housekeeper moving around. He opened the cellar door and went quickly down the steps.

The air had a cool musty smell. He switched on his flashlight and began to search the basement: oil burner, the winter's fireplace wood, neat rows of preserves and jams and pickles, a room filled with discarded furniture and unused jelly glasses, and one holding trunks, suitcases, and boxes of all kinds.

If the missing boxes were anywhere in the house they would be here. Jim moved fast. First he checked the boxes, but none were the right size, none bore the identifying mark. He was opening an old-fashioned trunk when an unshaded droplight flashed on. He whirled around, the top of the trunk slamming shut.

Abraham Allen stood facing him, holding a small revolver pointed at Jim's heart.

"Don't move," he said in his nasal voice, "or I'll shoot. Stand back against the wall. Raise your arms over your head."

Jim, raging at himself for being off guard, for letting himself be caught by Allen, of all men in the world, did as he was told. Only a fool argues with a loaded gun.

Allen looked him over in leisurely silence, eyes steady and cold as a fish, mouth drawn tightly in at the corners. A hard and unsympathetic man, Jim thought. But a courageous man.

"I've seen you before," Allen said at last. "Why, you are Roger Clayton's chauffeur."

"I am also," Jim said quietly, "Andrew Trevor's son."

There was a quick flash in the cold eyes. "So that explains it" Allen said nastily. "A thief like your father."

Jim dropped his arms, stepped forward.

"Don't move," Allen said sharply.

"I wasn't going to touch you," Jim said, and the contempt of his voice stung the older man. "I don't hit men old enough to be my father. But no one knows better than you, Honest Abe, that you are lying. Deliberately lying. You know my father made an honest mistake."

Allen smiled. His hand tightened on his revolver. "You can't frighten me and you can't talk your way out of this by trying to draw any red herrings across the path. I've caught you in the act."

"What act?" Jim asked coolly.

"Housebreaking. Robbery. Don't think for a moment that I won't expose you to Clayton."

"Exposing." Jim laughed. "That's about the best thing you do, isn't it, Honest Abe? If there is any exposing to be done, that's going to be my job," he added tightly. "I intend to expose you not merely to Clayton but to everyone in Mapleville. I want them to see you as you are. The man who deliberately blackened my father's name out of vindictive jealousy. Because you couldn't be the kind of man he is. You couldn't buy for yourself the kind of popularity he earned by his sheer kindness, his sheer goodness. You've let him spend four years in exile, in a private hell of his own." Jim's tongue lashed at Allen. "Why didn't you tell anyone that my father wanted to make restitution?"

Allen considered him for a moment. Then he said, frost in his voice, "To get back to the main point—why are you robbing my house, Trevor?"

"Put down that revolver, Honest Abe," Jim told him, and his biting scorn brought color into Allen's sallow face. "I won't attack you and I won't run away. Maybe this is best, after all."

Paying no attention to the small deadly weapon, he perched on the trunk and clasped his knee in his hands. Something in his relaxed manner made Allen put on the safety catch and drop the revolver in his pocket.

"That's better," Jim said coolly. "I wasn't robbing your house, Honest Abe—"

"Stop calling me that!" Allen's voice rasped as though he had been goaded beyond endurance.

"As you like. I understood that you were the one who gave yourself that sobriquet.

207

However — as I said, I didn't come here to rob you. I came to search this place."

"What are you looking for?"

"Some crates or boxes with a mark like this—" Jim drew the figure Φ. His eyes were fixed on Allen's face, but he could read nothing there but anger and bewilderment. "They were removed from the warehouse just a short time before it was set on fire."

"And what has all this to do with you?"

"Sorry. I can't tell you that."

"I'm not surprised," Allen sneered. "What am I supposed to have stolen from the warehouse?"

"I don't know," Jim admitted. "I have a theory. In fact, I'm damned sure that some of you governors of the Institute — perhaps all three of you working in cahoots — are systematically stealing the Bellamy collection and selling it for your own profit."

Allen leaned against the wall as though his legs had suddenly failed him. His small sharp eyes bored into Jim Trevor's like twin electric drills. There was a strange, strained expression on his sallow face. His features seemed to have sharpened.

"That," Jim went on deliberately, "would account for the savage attacks on Gillian Bellamy. With her out of the way, there would be no danger of a complete checkup of the collection being made. There would also be a great deal of money of which the governors would have almost unlimited use, unquestioned use."

Allen gave a bark of derisive laughter. "You're a young fool! Because Miss Bellamy happens to be an attractive girl, you've fallen for those hysterical stories of hers. There's not a word of truth in them."

"No?" Jim said softly, dangerously.

"No." Unexpectedly, Allen gave him a mocking smile. "I believe in facts—not schoolgirl dramatics. I'll give you some facts to work on. Gillian Bellamy's mother died insane, an insanity that had recurred in her family for at least four generations; possibly, if one had the complete records, even longer."

There was a long strained silence while the two men looked at each other. In Allen's voice there had been an unmistakable ring of truth. He smiled grimly as he saw the color fade out of Jim Trevor's lips.

"Now," Allen said, looking at Jim's white face, "get out of here and don't come back. And get this straight, I intend to tell Roger Clayton who you are."

"What an informer you would make,

Honest Abe," Jim said lazily. "It's almost a pity that Mr. Clayton already knows who I am. Such a waste of your talent!" He started toward the cellar stairs, turned back. "There's one thing I'd like to know. Why did you try to get into that burning warehouse, Mr. Allen? What were you looking for?"

"Damn it," Allen snapped, "I saw someone inside. I thought he was trapped. If I'd known who you were, I'd have been glad to see you burn."

"I'm sure of that," Jim said.

He went up the stairs, out into the fresh sweet air and the daylight.

Jill's mother insane! Four generations of madness. A terrible heritage. He knew that Allen believed what he had said, believed it without a trace of doubt.

Jill! The pain seemed to be more than he could bear. Then, as the first shock faded, Jim thought of the circumstances. Allen had used Jill's inherited madness as an explanation for the attacks on her. They were mere figments of her diseased imagination. But the attacks had really happened. Mad or sane, she had not imagined them. He had found her locked in the warehouse, he had found her unconscious beside it. Mrs. Meam had verified the first two accidents, the gas and the brakes that failed. She had been called in to nurse the girl.

Jim went striding along the road, his thoughts in a turmoil. He remembered the clear steady eyes, the sweet firm mouth, the transparent honesty, the gallant courage. No, he told himself. I don't believe it! I refuse to believe it. Forgive me, Jill. Jill, darling, forgive me. I'll never doubt you again.

He leaned against a stone fence and fumbled for his pipe. Odd, he must have left it in his room. He turned and saw the fence clearly, saw the locked gates, saw the sign: PENN MANOR — FOR SALE. For a long time, he stared up the driveway at the deserted house. Then, on impulse, he pulled out a heavy keyring and selected the big key that unlocked the gates. He pushed them wide open, creaking in protest on their rusty hinges, and walked slowly up the driveway.

He unlocked the front door. The house was unexpectedly cool. The drawn shades made it dark. He went briskly into the great drawing room on the right to raise shades and fling open the windows to the light and air.

The furnishings had been left as they were, the magnificent Oriental rugs, the eighteenth-century French furniture. Only the oil painting of Jim's mother, which had hung over the fireplace, was gone. His father had taken that with him.

To his surprise there was no trace of dust, no indication indoors, as there was outside, that the house had long been unoccupied. His father had left no one as caretaker but someone had been looking after it. Sally Meam, of course! Even though she had been one of those who had lost their savings in the oil deal, she had continued to keep Andrew Trevor's house spotless for him—her way of thanking him for the heavy hospital bills he had paid when she had had a serious illness.

Jim went through the two-story library, with its circular staircase that led up to his father's bedroom, and nearly ten thousand books filling the shelves. Andrew Trevor had taken with him only a handful of his favorite books. From the library, Jim went through the small sitting room beyond, with its furniture covered in bright chintz, and then crossed the wide foyer to the formal dining room with its high carved Spanish chairs and superb refectory table, through the small informal dining room to the big modern kitchen.

The sight of the kitchen reminded him that he had had no lunch. He'd better be on his way. He could come back another time. Then he remembered that he had set out this morning to follow the possible track of the stolen pick-up truck, to find where the missing boxes had been hidden.

If someone had chosen Penn Manor because it was unoccupied, he'd hardly have gone upstairs. Better try the basement first. Jim ran down the stairs, stopped short. At the foot of the stairs were stacked seven boxes. Each of them was marked with an Φ.

While he stood staring at them he heard someone walking overhead. Someone in the house! The man who had hidden the boxes? Who else could it be?

Jim moved purposefully toward a woodpile, selected a small but stout stick and crept up the stairs. He stepped into the kitchen — and stopped.

Standing with her back to him, opening a picnic lunch on the kitchen table, was Gillian Bellamy.

XVIII

"Where on earth have you been?" Mrs. Bennett said petulantly as Jill went up to her room. "The phone's been ringing for you constantly. There are a sheaf of messages downstairs. Sometimes I think every eligible man in town thinks he has to call you at least once a day."

Jill laughed. "Sorry they've been a nuisance. I've been at the Institute."

"I might have known."

From the open door of the Bennett's bedroom, Mr. Bennett called, "Gillian? Come in, my dear."

"Oh, William," Mrs. Bennett said in her fretful voice, "I don't think she really ought to. The doctor said you were to keep perfectly quiet."

"I didn't ask her to do the twist with me, Maud! I just asked her to come in and chat

214

with me for a few minutes. It's dull just lying here."

"Well, if you think it's all right — I'll go down and see about lunch. The house has been so upset I haven't made out my menus."

"Don't bother about lunch for me," Jill said quickly. "It's a lovely day. I'll fix a picnic lunch and take it out somewhere."

With a harassed air, Mrs. Bennett let her in the bedroom. "Now don't tire him or excite him," she warned the girl. She sighed and went downstairs, as usual carrying with her a conviction that life was too much for her and that she had more burdens than a woman could bear.

William Bennett was propped up on pillows in the big bed. His face had a gray tone but his lips had lost their blue look. He summoned up a smile for Jill and waved her toward a chair.

"You look so much better," she assured him.

"Let's not fool ourselves," he told her. "That was a bad attack this morning. Very bad. Heaven knows how long I'll be stuck in bed now." His fist clenched and he beat it in exasperation against the headboard. Let it drop helplessly on the blanket cover. "Why did it have to happen now, of all times!"

"You mustn't excite yourself," Jill warned him. "All you are supposed to do is rest and vegetate and get well. Fortunately, Chester is still on vacation. He can take your place at the Institute. In fact, he is there now."

"Chester — at — the — Institute?" Bennett spoke in a series of short breaths.

Jill nodded brightly, thinking it would ease the tension between father and son if he knew that Chester was trying to help.

"They are checking Dad's catalogue against the card files. Chester was working his head off. Some of the pages seem to be missing."

"No!" Bennett's cry was a frenzied shout.

"Please, Mr. Bennett," Jill exclaimed, shocked by the sick man's expression. "Please don't get upset."

"Gillian!" Mrs. Bennett cried as she ran into the room. "I told you not to excite him! Go away at once and don't come back to this room until William has recovered enough to get up."

Jill had planned to eat her lunch under the trees beside the little fern-edged pool which had first attracted her attention at Penn Manor. To her surprise, the iron gates stood wide open. As though they were prepared to welcome me, Jill thought. She followed the

216

driveway, turned off the motor in front of the long flight of stairs that led to the entrance, and took up her picnic basket. The front door, as she half expected by this time, opened at her touch. As though the house awaited its new owner and welcomed her in.

Carrying the picnic basket, she went through the two dining rooms and into the big sunlit kitchen. This house was meant to be lived in. What a pity it should ever have been vacant.

She set the basket on the table, began to take out sandwiches, cake, deviled eggs, pickles, and the thermos of lemonade. There was even a neatly folded tablecloth.

A sound made her whirl around, her heart in her throat. She stared at the tall man who stood in the cellar doorway, looking at her. It seemed as though his eyes read clear into her soul. Then he nodded his head.

"I knew it," he said as though to himself. "I was sure of it."

"Peter! You startled me."

"I'm sorry. Let me help you with that." He unpacked the basket and set the table. "Are you having a party?"

She explained about her guardian's heart attack and why it had seemed simpler to take out a picnic basket for her lunch.

He grinned boyishly. "You must have a very healthy appetite."

Unexpectedly, Jill felt shy with him, remembering Denise's public attempt to humiliate him. "Would you care to share my lunch?"

"The Clayton chauffeur," he reminded her gravely. "I shouldn't want to cause you any embarrassment with my employers."

Jill forgot her temporary shyness. "I choose my own friends," she said quietly. "It would embarrass me only if I had to repeat my invitation."

"Thank you." He pulled out her chair for her and drew up another for himself.

For a while they ate hungrily, without attempting to talk. Then, after they had had a second piece of cake and they did not even want any more lemonade, Jill sat back and looked around the big kitchen.

"My first meal in this house," she said.

Something flamed behind his eyes. "Your first?"

"I want to buy Penn Manor and make it my home. For all my life. I want to be rooted deep in America. Someday I may travel again, but only for short visits. I want to be a part of this. I want it to be a part of me."

"So do I," he said huskily.

He smiled suddenly, the smile of whose charm he was so completely unaware. He leaned forward and with a finger tip gently tilted up her chin so that her eyes met his. For a long moment they looked deeply into hers.

Then he said, very quietly, "You came into this house and found me prowling around. You haven't asked me any questions."

"They aren't necessary," Jill said softly.

"Oh, Jill, my—" He broke off, dropped the hands that had reached for hers.

Jill folded on her lap the shaking hands that had gone out so spontaneously to take the ones he had held to her. Somehow, somewhere, there was a barrier between them, something that made him withdraw the hands that had reached for hers. Someday, perhaps, it would fall of its own accord. Meantime she must wait.

"Penn Manor is for sale," she said at last, when her voice was steady. "I talked to the governors about it this morning. They didn't seem to approve of the idea, but I can't afford to wait. Mr. Clayton says there is plenty of time, but by the time I'm twenty-one someone else may have snatched it away. I can't bear it. If only the owner would be willing to wait until I'm of age! I could call the real estate people and find out who he is."

"The owner is a man named Andrew Trevor," Jim told her.

"Andrew Trevor! Queer how his name keeps cropping up, isn't it?"

"Does his name keep cropping up?"

At his sharp tone Jill laughed. "Hey, don't bark at me like that."

"Sorry. But what do you know about Andrew Trevor?"

Jill repeated the comments she had heard exchanged between Roger Clayton and Abraham Allen, and what Mrs. Meam had told her.

"Aunt Sally lost everything she had saved in the oil swindle; that's why she has to go on renting out rooms. But what hurts her most is losing her faith in Mr. Trevor. She thought he was the best man she had ever known. She liked his son, too, though she said she was afraid he had neglected his sick father because he was just about off his head over Denise Clayton."

"I expect a lot of people have been in the same state at one time or another," he said coolly. "But it's like catching cold. They get over it."

Jill looked at him swiftly and away. "Do they?"

"I suppose you've guessed—I loved her,"

he said steadily. "It was a boy's first love. The kind of love one can give only once."

Jill felt as though a giant hand had squeezed her heart. After all, what had she expected? Denise was distractingly pretty. She had qualities that would attract any man. Look at what she was doing now to Chester.

She got up hastily and began to repack the picnic basket with hands that trembled.

"Yes, I know. I—heard Denise say so one night. I didn't mean to eavesdrop. But—"

"But there is another kind of love," Jim said. He stood beside her, looking down. His voice was quiet, tender. "A man's love. The love that endures and burns like a steady flame after the fever of a boy's infatuation has gone out. The only real love. I never had that to give to Denise."

Jill's heart leaped in her breast. Her breath came fast. Unexpectedly, his hand covered hers.

"Wait a little, Jill. As Mr. Clayton says, there's plenty of time. There's a bright future for—for you." Laughter edged his words. "I read it in the tea leaves. And in my crystal ball I see you living in this house, filling it with sunshine even on the darkest days, with children around you and a—an adoring husband."

"What a wonderful fortune teller you are."
She tried to speak lightly, to cover her confusion. She looked up to see his eyes smiling at her.

"You like the fortune?"

"It's—perfect."

"And what about the fortune teller? No words of approval for him?"

She remembered Dan Holt's words. *He's got something any woman would fall for.* And Denise's warning. *That's his stock in trade.*

"You ought to make a profession of it," she said lightly. She dared not look at him, afraid her eyes would betray her. "Let's explore the house. Do you know what I'd like to do? Give a dinner party here and cook the meal myself."

"Why not?"

"Well, there's no electricity for lights and stove and refrigeration."

"I'll see the real estate people and arrange it," Jim said. "I'll also ask them to hold up the sale of Penn Manor."

"Peter! Do you think they would?"

"I think they would," he said gravely, but with a glint of humor in his eyes. "But before you explore the house I have something to show you. And before that, I have something to tell you—to lead up to the grand climax."

He fumbled in his pockets. "Darn! I keep forgetting that I left my pipe at home."

Jill opened her handbag and handed him the broken pieces of his pipe. "Is this it?"

"Where on earth did you find that?"

"In the Claytons' swimming pool this morning."

"So that's what happened! Then I had better tell you how it got there."

He described how he had decided to look for the boxes that had been removed from the warehouse before the fire, and how he planned to start by searching the Bennett garage.

"Because gas from my car was probably used to start the fire."

"Smart gal. Got it in one." He went on to repeat the conversation he had overheard and how he had been thrown into the pool to keep him from identifying the two men.

"So that was it!" Jill released her breath in a long sigh of relief. "Last night, I saw you standing in your window with a—with a revolver. I was terribly worried. So that— Peter! That man who talked about hiding. Do you think he could possibly have been John Jones?"

"I'm dead sure of it."

"Peter!" She caught hold of his arm. "What is this all about? Have you any idea?"

"Don't look so little and frightened. You're all eyes." He laughed unsteadily.

"I'm neither scared nor helpless," she retorted. "But I am bewildered. I don't understand any of this. Not at all. Do you?"

"I think I do," he said slowly. "I haven't a scrap of proof. But I have a strong suspicion that everything that has happened is tied in with the Bellamy Institute."

Jill frowned. "But what would that man Jones have to do with the Institute?"

"I'm not sure. But I'd be willing to make a fairly large bet that something is wrong in the way the Institute is being managed."

"The Praxiteles bust," Jill said quickly, "and the missing pages of the catalogue."

"What catalogue?" Jim asked quickly.

Jill told him about the governors and Chester checking the catalogue that morning. Some pages were missing. The Praxiteles bust was not listed on the pages they had.

"So I was right!" There was a triumphant gleam in Jim Trevor's eyes. "But what was Chester Bennett doing there?"

Jill explained that he had apparently gone to replace his father to make up for the quarrel that had caused his father's heart attack. There had been something wrong between them for some time. Mr. Bennett seemed to be keeping an eye on his son, to be worried about him.

She looked up to find him watching her speculatively. She was very cool in speaking of the man she was engaged to marry, he thought. Surely she could not be in love with him.

"We'll see whether we can produce some evidence," he said. "Just follow me, madam."

"Evidence of what?"

"Evidence to back up my theory that someone is systematically robbing the Institute of its treasures."

"Oh, no," Jill protested. "That's impossible. The governors are men whom my father trusted implicitly."

"Just the same, someone took those boxes out of the warehouse. And what's more—I've found them."

"Where?"

Jim saw her startled face. His tone became facetious, imitating the stage magician.

"If you will look closely, ladies and gentlemen, you will see that I have nothing concealed up my sleeves, no rabbits in my hat. Now, when I wave my wand—"

He picked up the stick he had brought

from the basement, flourished it, led her down the stairs, and waved the stick with a dramatic gesture at the boxes. Jill stood staring at them, saw the mark she had noticed when she was locked in the small office at the warehouse.

"Recognize them?" he asked.

She nodded mutely. "How on earth did you do it?"

He showed her the map he had drawn after discovering the number of miles the stolen truck had been driven. The cache had to be close at hand. He had checked every possible place until he reached Penn Manor. An unoccupied house. It must have seemed perfectly safe.

"But how did he get the boxes in here? The gates were locked."

"Over the stone fence. It's very low. That would be easy enough."

"What are you going to do, Peter?"

"The question is—what do you want me to do? If I am right about it, these cases contain stolen pictures or sculpture from the Institute. They belong to you."

Jill bit her lip in indecision. Then she said, "Let's find out."

Jim nodded, went to the toolroom for a chisel and opened the top box. Carefully he lifted out the crumpled paper and excelsior that held the contents firm and reached in, then dug out a rolled canvas. He opened it carefully.

"It's a Picasso," Jill said. "There were two of that cubist period."

"So I was right," Jim said softly. He dug deeper, pulled out another canvas.

"A Matisse," Jill identified it quickly. "Why—" She crouched on the floor beside it, frowning. "Let's take them both up into the light."

When they were spread on the table, Jill studied them intently.

"The Picasso seems to be all right," she said in relief. "But I'm not sure. I've got a horrible fear that these are both—"

"Both what?"

"Copies. The Matisse is a copy of the painting my father owned. But what does this mean? One original, one copy."

"I think it means that some originals were removed and were sold or are about to be sold. But those must be items that appeared on the few missing pages. Where the catalogue pages could not be removed, paintings have been copied, and I suspect the copies were to be substituted in the Institute and the originals sold to collectors who would not

227

worry too much about the provenance of the paintings. Or it's possible the originals are to be kept and copies sold to gullible buyers who won't know the difference."

"What a beastly, criminal thing to do!" Jill said hotly. "But what has John Jones to do with all this—if anything?"

"You remember Mrs. Meam said he had lived abroad a lot. Want to bet he's a painter, the man who was making the copies, working in that locked part of the warehouse with its shining clean windows? He'd have a good north light there."

"Could be. Who was back of this, Peter? I've got to know. Which one of the governors has been defrauding my father?"

"I don't know," he admitted. "I can't even guess. I need to know a lot more about them as men, their financial position, their record for honest dealing, whether they've been known to yield to temptation in the past."

"What shall we do with these boxes? If we leave them here, they will be taken away, hidden somewhere else, or sold, and we'll never find them again. Because the governors know now that I've discovered Penn Manor, that I'm interested in it, and that probably I have gone all over the place."

"I have an idea," he said. "I'll move them

to an attic room and put on a lock that can't be broken. Leave it to me. And, Jill—"

"Yes?"

"When you give that dinner party of yours here at Penn Manor, ask all the governors, will you? Someone is going to be mighty anxious about these boxes. Look—here's another idea. Ask them to dinner and then, at the last moment, too late for them to do anything about it, tell them you have decided to have it here."

"But suppose someone—suppose something happens?"

"I hope to heaven it does. And don't worry," he told her. "I'll be here."

XIX

From his window above the garage Jim watched Dan Holt floating in the pool while Denise lay in a long chair in her bathing suit, her gold hair in soft curls on her head, a tall frosty drink in her slim hand with its long pointed nails.

He felt only detached interest in the lovely picture she made. His golden girl had turned to dross. Nothing she could do or say would ever again have power to hurt him.

In contrast, he thought of Jill, eating her picnic lunch unselfconsciously in the kitchen at Penn Manor; her gracious insistence that he be her guest, though she knew only of his present position; that moment of adorable shyness before she spoke. He thought how she had caught him searching the house and had asked no questions. She had given him blind trust as he had given her his faith, even after hearing Allen's ugly accusation.

Someday, please God, she would know she did not love Chester Bennett. Someday he would clear his father and he could come to her, a free man with a clean name to offer her. And he would ask his father to give her Penn Manor for a wedding present. How Andrew Trevor would love having this girl for a daughter-in-law.

Hey, hold it, he warned himself, you're taking a lot for granted. You haven't won her yet.

After moving the boxes to an attic room, he had bought a strong padlock for the door and then stopped to see the real estate man who handled the house for his father. It was to be taken off the market, he instructed him.

Roger Clayton had told him that his services would not be needed that day. The older man had given him an anxious look, but Jim had not made any report. There was a great deal he wanted to know about Clayton before he could trust him completely.

Now he went down the stairs and around the garage to keep out of Denise's line of vision. He heard her light voice say, "Dan, there's Chester sitting over there all alone. Let's have him join us for a swim or a drink or something."

"Let him alone, Denise," he said lazily.

She laughed softly. "Afraid I'll break up his romance with little Gillian? She'll have to learn that a woman's main job is not getting her man, it's keeping him." She raised her voice. "Chester! Yoohoo! Come on in. The water's fine."

There was a joyous hail from the Bennett terrace and the sound of running feet.

Jim's lips tightened. But it was no concern of his. If Chester was such a fool as to prefer Denise to Jill he was asking for punishment. If only Jill wouldn't be hurt by it!

He darted behind the shrubbery and slipped out into the street. He missed the Thunderbird his father had given him on his last birthday and which was eating its head off in a New York garage.

He reached the office of the Mapleville *Gazette* a little after five, a one-story brick house that had been converted into a newspaper and printing office. Only one person was still in the building, an elderly man, coatless, a green eyeshade pushed up on his forehead.

He peered at Jim. "What can I do for you, young man?"

"I'd like to see some back issues of the paper. The last two weeks should be enough."

"Guess that's possible." The editor pulled out some copies of the paper, slapped dust out of them, and laid them before Jim.

It took almost no time to find the item he was seeking: MASTERPIECE ACQUIRED BY NEW OWNER . . .

Jim pulled out a pencil and paper and wrote down: *Hendrick Freelton, Cincinnati, Ohio, The Man with the Broken Nose, Praxiteles.*

He handed back the papers. "Thanks very much."

The elderly man took off his eyeshade. "I think I could put a name to you," he said slowly.

Jim's face was blank.

"You're Andy Trevor's boy."

For a moment neither man spoke.

"You know," the editor said in a leisurely way, "I thought a lot of your dad. He was just about the best thing ever happened to this village. Many's the time he has sat in that very chair and we'd chew the rag, talking about what could be done for Mapleville, swapping ideas about ways and means. I never see that empty house of his but I get mad all over again.

"You know, son, this place didn't deserve Andy and that's a fact. There's something all wrong in that muck Honest Abe Allen handed out about your dad rooking people. Oh, sure, he got taken in and he made an honest mistake. Who doesn't? Show me someone who never made a mistake and I'll show you a monster."

"I'm glad to hear you say that, Mr.—"

"Loomis. Just tell Andy that Ted Loomis sent him his best and said it's high time he came back here where he belongs."

He held out a bony hand to Jim, who took it in a hard grasp. "I'll tell him," he said huskily. "It will give him a lot of pleasure."

"What's he doing with himself these days?"

"Breaking his heart," Jim told him bluntly.

"Sit back, son, and tell me about him. The paper's been put to bed and nothing to do now. I kind of miss talking to Andy when the day's work is done."

Jim talked for a long time. When he had finished Loomis was beaming.

"Well now," he said, "well, now! I don't know when I've been more pleased. Between us, son, we're going to cook Honest Abe's goose and clear your father. For four years I've been wanting to wipe that smug, sanctimonious look off Allen's face. You tell your father to start packing up because he's on his way back to Mapleville with a brass band to meet him. No, dang it, give me Andy's address and I'll write him myself!"

Jim was smiling when he left the office of the *Gazette,* warmed by Loomis's hearty handshake, hearing in his ears the man's friendly voice. He felt lighter-hearted than he had at any time since he reached Mapleville. Now at last he felt that he was not alone in his plans to clear his father. He had the stanch support of a firm friend whose faith in Andrew Trevor's integrity was as unshakable as his own. A man who was willing to fight for what he believed in, as well as to talk about it.

Jim still did not know which, if any, of the governors could be cleared of suspicion of robbing the Institute. From day to day, Clayton had looked more anxious. There had been a queer trapped expression on Honest Abe's face when Jim had told him his suspicions. Bennett had had a heart attack because of some very heated argument with his son. Then Chester had taken advantage of his father's illness to go to the Institute.

All of them, then, working together? But in that case, why had Clayton informed Garrison of Gillian Bellamy's "accidents"? So that he would appear to be in the clear, no matter what happened?

Jim frowned. What he needed now was to talk to Garrison, tell him what he had learned and ask his advice. But where could he make his call? The telephones in Mapleville were nearly all on party lines. He could not call from the Claytons' private wire without the risk of being overheard, on one of the extensions, by someone in the house.

He went swiftly down the street and paused at the door of Sally Meam's shabby house. His heart pinched as he thought of this trusting woman, hardworking and kindly, who had lost her savings. He vowed to see that his father reimbursed her within a week. At least that much could be set right without any further delay.

There was a mouth-watering smell of baking bread. Mrs. Meam flung open the door.

"May I come in?"

"Of course. I got behind with my baking today. One jiffy and I'll have it out of the oven. I've got a nice nourishing vegetable soup, and a lobster newburg planned for tonight. Hot rolls fresh out of the oven and a strawberry shortcake. Enough for four and there's only Miss Thompkins. Will you stay?"

Jim grinned, amused. "It suits me right down to the ground. But how about your lodger?"

"Where else can she eat like that?" Mrs. Meam demanded. "I noticed she came back as mad as hops last night." She added hopefully, "Have a fight?"

"She found out I was a chauffeur and she didn't like it."

Mrs. Meam hesitated, her kindly face troubled. "Jim, it's none of my business why you are here or what you are doing. When you came to see me that first day and told me you were staying here under another name I promised I wouldn't give you away. I haven't. Not even to Gillian Bellamy, though when you showed up with her I nearly fell over. Only I've just got to say it. I hope you're not still—that is, I guess you're in love, aren't you?"

"Head over heels. Absolutely. Forever," he told her. "Now may I use your telephone for some long-distance calls?"

"Sure. It's still a private wire and I've got that booth with a door on it for my lodgers. No one can overhear you. Help yourself."

After a struggle with the long-distance operator, Jim reached Hendrick Freelton in Cincinnati. He told his story succinctly. Then he held the telephone away from his ears while the Ohio art collector let loose a blast of sheer rage.

When he had run out of breath, Jim asked what he intended to do.

"I'll come East as soon as I can get away and I'll clear this up if it's the last thing I ever do. I've built one of the finest private collections in this country and there's never been a question about a single item in it. Stolen goods! If you're right, I intend to make someone sweat for this."

"Thank you, sir. That's good news. I'm expecting to see some fireworks."

"Fireworks!" snorted the irate collector. "If there's anything wrong with that Praxiteles bust you're going to see Vesuvius in action."

Jim was grinning to himself as he dialed Garrison's unlisted home number in New York. Things were beginning to move at last.

"Well, Trevor," Garrison said eagerly, "how are you making out up there? Have you picked up any ideas?"

"Quite a few, sir. Is it convenient for you to listen now? This may take some time."

"There's nothing more urgent, more important. Take as long as you like."

Jim wondered whether one secret of Garrison's success was not his ability to give an impression of leisure, however much work he might have to get through.

"I must say," Garrison told him, "I didn't like what that insurance fellow, Hartman, told me about the fire on that piece of property of Miss Bellamy's. Warehouse, wasn't it?"

"Yes."

"How did it strike you? Part of the same picture?"

Jim had already marshaled his facts and he gave them as quickly as possible, leaving out nothing, and ending with a summary of his own conclusions.

There was a thoughtful pause when he had finished. Then Garrison surprised him. He chuckled.

"It's the Wicks case all over again. Left to your own devices you choose unorthodox methods but you certainly get results. I foresee a big future for you, Trevor."

"Thank you, sir."

"Now I'll give you what our investigators have managed to dig up from the New York end. Roger Clayton seems to be in financial difficulties. He has overextended and his colleagues are getting badly worried. Some of them are already trying to pull out before they lose their shirts."

"Well, well," Jim said softly.

"Abraham Allen appears to be solidly

fixed. He'll never be in danger of overextending, from all accounts. He's careful of spending a penny. Reputation for being ambitious but very cautious. He edges his way, a step at a time."

"Uh-huh."

"William Bennett is retired. Sold his New York gallery to a fellow named Noonan, Oliver Noonan. He can't attract the same caliber of established artists that Bennett had but he seems to be doing nicely with younger painters at lower prices. Quantity sales rather than quality."

"So," Jim said thoughtfully, "Clayton is the one who needs the money."

"Looks like it. Looks like it. I'm surprised, frankly. I've known him for years and he struck me as having his feet on the ground. Well, keep in touch, my boy, and if you need any help we can supply from New York don't hesitate to call on us."

Jim put down the telephone. Mrs. Meam was arranging fresh-cut flowers in a vase in her old-fashioned sitting room. He put his arm around her and gave her an affectionate hug.

"Don't you ever rest?"

"I like fresh flowers," she said practically in her cheerful voice, "and they aren't going to walk in here by themselves, that I've ever noticed. Somebody has to pick them. You're losing weight, Jim? You'd better let me start feeding you."

"Suppose Penn Manor should be opened up again," he said suddenly. "Would you like to go back there as the housekeeper? You'd have enough staff so all you'd have to do would be the directing."

Her round pleasant face flushed uncomfortably. She smoothed her apron, avoiding his eyes.

"We-ell," she began, embarrassed, "I'm doing right well on my own. I'm kind of used to it now."

"There's something I want to tell you about my father," he said quietly. "But first—I want to know exactly how much money you lost through that oil swindle he was involved in."

The kindly face was troubled. "Eight thousand dollars," she said reluctantly.

"That money should have been returned to you before now," Jim said. "It will come at once. My father wanted it to be returned long ago. He did his best to make restitution but Mr. Allen told him no one here would have any further dealings with him."

"No one ever knew that," Mrs. Meam said.

241

"Mr. Allen didn't tell anyone, or I'd have heard about it. In fact, he was the one said your father had made money out of that deal."

She lifted her head. "Did you hear something? Oh, I guess it was just the kids next door. But I'm mighty happy to know about it. Not just the money. Only I trusted your father and that's why it hurt especially."

"I know," Jim said gruffly.

"You mean he's really got enough money now to pay back? That he can afford it?"

"More than enough. He's a wealthy man now."

She touched his arm. "Jim?"

"Yes?"

"You meant it about reopening Penn Manor?"

"Yes."

"With—a lady of the house?"

"I hope so."

"You never got over her, did you? Oh, Jim! How can you be so blind! Denise Clayton will spoil your life again just the way she did four years ago."

"Well," Lola Thompkins said brightly from the doorway, "if it isn't the Clayton chauffeur!"

"I've asked him to stay to dinner," Mrs.

Meam said flatly.

Lola looked at Jim with a malicious triumph that disturbed him. Not a kitten this time. A tiger crouching to spring.

"Sorry," he said abruptly. "Not tonight. Another time, if I may."

He turned and went out of the house. Behind him he heard the sound of Lola's mocking laughter.

She turned to Mrs. Meam. "So you knew all the time that he was Jim Trevor and not Peter Carr," she accused the older woman.

"Of course. I was his father's housekeeper when he lived here at Penn Manor."

"That's odd. Mr. Trevor never spoke of coming from Connecticut. In fact, he never mentioned the past."

"He had a lot of trouble here," Mrs. Meam explained. "He was gullible, I guess, and half the town lost most of its savings on his oil —"

"Swindle?" Lola said smoothly.

"So you were listening at the door. I thought I heard someone. I don't like snoopers in my house, Miss Thompkins. And I can tell you one thing. Jim says his father is going to pay it all back! He's a rich man now and he always was an honest one."

Lola laughed. "Poor Mrs. Meam! First you

were taken in by the father and now by the son."

"What on earth do you mean?"

"I mean," Lola said shrilly, "that I knew Jim and his father out West. Jim is lying to you. His father has no money. He's just a roustabout at the oilfields. No one has the slightest use for him. And after tonight you can have my room. I'm going home tomorrow!"

XX

The note, with the rest of her mail, lay beside her plate at the breakfast table. It was addressed to Miss Gillian Bellamy, but it was unstamped. It must have been delivered by hand. The writing, bold and square, was strange to her, and yet Jill was sure she knew the sender. She slipped it in the huge patch pocket of her corn-colored wrap-around skirt. She did not want to read it now with Chester's eyes on her.

When she looked up she saw, as she expected, that he was watching her. Until his mother went upstairs to see whether her husband needed anything, he had been studiously polite.

"I like that brown shirt with the yellow skirt," he had said. "Nice colors with your hair, bring out the copper glints in it. Very fetching."

"Glad you like them. I didn't know you were interested in color combinations, Chester. That's something new for you, isn't it?"

"Denise wears a lot of yellow," Chester had said, and then he had concentrated on his waffles and sausage.

But when his mother had gone he looked at Jill in a different way. She felt the unopened letter burning a hole in her pocket. Was that what interested him? She met his eyes and her own opened wide, startled, shocked by what they saw.

"Chester! What's wrong? You look at me as though you hated me."

"Why did you deliberately upset Dad, Jill? You knew he'd just had a heart attack. Why did you tell him about the missing pages of the catalogue and stir him up the way you did? You might have killed him."

"I never knew you could be so unfair," she stormed. "I was only trying to cheer him up, to let him know how much you were doing to help him by working at the Institute in his place. I never meant to upset him. I didn't dream it would be such a shock to him."

"Sorry," he mumbled. "I apologize, Jill. I guess I'm upset myself. Dad's in bad shape and he shouldn't be bothered by anything.

You're right though. I wasn't fair. If only," he groaned despairingly, "you had promised to marry me, Jill, everything would have been all right."

Jill set down her coffee cup and faced him squarely, spots of color burning in her cheeks.

"Look here, Chester, you are all mixed up. You know that, don't you? If you don't you had better start thinking—hard. First you blame me for telling your father about the missing pages of the catalogue. Next you blame me for not having promised to marry you. You can't live like that, shifting the blame, shifting the responsibility to someone else."

He met her stormy eyes, looked away.

"You aren't being honest with yourself, Chester, and that's not like you. I didn't cause your father's heart attack. That grew out of your own quarrel with him. So far as my marrying you is concerned, you know I don't love you. I'm fond of you but that's not enough. Not enough for me. Not enough for you."

She forced him to look at her. "And what's more, Chester Bennett, you're in love with Denise Clayton and you know it! To try to marry me, in the circumstances, is—just

—plain—cheating."

She pushed back her chair and went out of the room so quickly that he did not even have time to get to his feet. He looked after her and then got up, hands clenching and un-clenching. What am I going to do, he wondered.

Jill went out on the terrace, walking up and down because she was too angry to keep still. She pulled out the unstamped letter.

Hendrick Freelton is coming here to Mapleville to find out the truth about the Praxiteles bust he bought. Don't mention this to *anyone*. He is pawing the ground with rage over having been tricked into buying stolen goods, so prepare for the battle of the century.

You're dining with the Claytons tonight, I know. If possible, slip out to meet me by the pool around nine-thirty. I have something to ask you.

From now on, keep your bedroom door locked.

Your
Peter

Jill looked more closely at the signature. Surely he had meant to write "Yours."

In the four days that had passed since her impromptu picnic at Penn Manor, Jill had seen Peter Carr only at a distance. They had been busy days. She had had several interviews with Mr. Loomis while they prepared for the first meeting of the Good Citizens League, as they had decided to call it. The meeting was to be held on the evening of July the Fourth in the main room of the Institute.

While Jill dressed for the dinner party with the Claytons she thought about Abraham Allen's hostility. So far, he had opposed every request that she had made to the governors. He did not want her to have a hand in founding the Good Citizens League. He did not want her to buy Penn Manor. He did not want her to be informed about the mismanagement of the Institute. He was less like a governor than a dictator, she thought in exasperation.

Jill fastened around her slim throat the fabulous pendant of rubies that had been part of the Bellamy collection. It provided a spectacular contrast with the jade-green dress, with its full diaphanous skirt, her gleaming arms and shoulders. The magnificent stones glowed against her skin. How terribly her mother had wanted those rubies! For a moment she shut her eyes in pain.

The Bellamy jewels belonged to the Bellamy heiress, her father had said grimly.

The Bellamy heiress! Jill thought of Denise's avid but mocking eyes. Impulsively she removed the glittering pendant and returned it to the jewel case. She chose a small pearl necklace instead, and adjusted pearl earrings.

Chester was waiting for her at the foot of the stairs. He whistled when he caught sight of her.

"You're beautiful, tonight! Absolutely radiant."

In the distance as they strolled across the lawn she heard the church chimes. "Only seven-fifteen," she said in surprise. "We're a quarter of an hour ahead of time."

Lights streamed out from the Clayton house. There was a blast of dance music from a record player.

"Turn that thing down, Denise," Clayton's big voice rang out irritably.

"I was just trying out a record," said the high sweet voice. "We are going to dance in the gameroom tonight after dinner. I got two dozen records by good name bands today. Simply marvelous dance music. That ought to be enough."

"Two dozen! Did you pay for them out

of your allowance?"

Denise laughed. "It took my whole allowance to pay part of last month's bills. I'm flat broke again and the month has just started. Dad, you'll simply have to step up my allowance. I just can't manage on it."

"You'll have to do better. I'm not going to raise it. I'm going to cut it."

"Dad! You can't do that!" The voice was shrill now. "You can't shut off every pleasure in life," she added sullenly.

"Every pleasure! The more you have the more you want. It's got to stop. I'm cutting your allowance in half, and you won't get the next installment until August first." His voice rose above her protest. "And if you don't pay your own bills for clothes after this, I'll stop your charge accounts. Business is bad. Very bad. I'm in a tight spot and I can't afford this constant drain on my income. Is that clear?"

There were twelve young couples, seated at tables for four in the big gameroom. Denise had discarded her favorite gold for the evening and wore a dress of flaming red tulle. There had been no trace of the recent quarrel with her father in her manner as she greeted them. As usual, she gushed over Chester. Her eyes narrowed as she saw Jill's dress, noticed

251

the glow in her face that made her breath-takingly beautiful.

"You look like a tulip," Chester told Denise huskily.

Dan Holt claimed Jill, his eyes bright as he looked at her radiant face.

"I'm going to have my work cut out, I can see that," he said. "Keeping you to myself. But I'm a man who likes a challenge."

Jill knew that she looked her best. Happiness had brought out the latent beauty in her eyes and lips, made her skin glow. She was perfectly well aware, too, that the happiness was due to the fact that in a little while, a couple of hours, she would be seeing Peter again.

Through the dinner, from iced melon balls to guinea hen and wild rice to the flaming dessert, talk and laughter were tossed gaily back and forth from table to table.

Then, when the tables had been cleared, Dan pushed back the rugs and started the record player. Jill looked up at the cuckoo clock. Only nine o'clock. Too early to meet Peter. How was she going to get away? The French windows in the gameroom opened on a flagged terrace. Garden chairs were set out with small iron tables. A tall lilac hedge shut off the terrace from the back of the house and the swimming pool.

As usual, she was besieged by partners. She could move only a few steps before she was claimed by someone else. Dan, in his role of host, was manfully dancing with the only wallflower, but his eyes followed the girl in the jade-green dress, with the burnished auburn hair and the glowing face.

Unspoiled and unselfconscious, she was able to have a good time without trying to attract attention. Denise moved like a flame, her gestures exaggerated, her laughter too sweet, her eyes too admiring as she tried to captivate each of her partners.

The cuckoo shot out and spoke briefly. Nine-thirty. At last. Dan was at the turntable. Quickly Jill slipped outside and ran around the lilac hedge toward the pool. No one there. She stopped abruptly.

Then from beside the lilac hedge a shadow moved and a man said quietly, "Here I am."

She ran straight toward him, both hands outstretched. He held them in his, strong and warm.

"I came as soon as I could."

"Sh-h-h." He drew her away from the lilac hedge and the terrace, closer to the swimming pool, still holding her hands. "No one is likely to hear us here. Thanks for coming."

"You knew I would come."

"I—hoped you would." His hands tightened spasmodically and then he released her, stepping back, breathing quickly.

The air was fragrant with the scent of roses. The stars were so big and bright it seemed as though she could touch them. She tilted her head back, looking at the glory of the sky.

His voice brought her back to earth with a thump. "Jill, my dar—" He cleared his throat. "Jill, do you know anything about Roger Clayton's finances?"

Whatever she had expected him to ask her, this was not it. She stared at him in astonishment.

"Is he hard up?" Jim asked, as though she might not have understood him.

"Why—" She brought her attention back to his question. "Why I think he is. Tonight, I heard—" She stopped short.

"What is it?"

"Peter, I—I can't."

"What's wrong?" His voice steadied her, supported her as though his arm were around her.

"Tonight I'm a guest in his house. I can't discuss him behind his back. It's treacherous."

"My sweet, loyal girl—" He made himself stop, but then he went on. "Look here, Jill, if he is in the clear you can't hurt him. If he is not in the clear you should not try to help him. Right?"

She hesitated. Then she capitulated a little reluctantly. "Right."

She told him of the conversation she had overheard between Roger Clayton and Denise about her allowance and her extravagance, which he could no longer afford. He was, he had said, in "a tight spot."

Jim grunted once but otherwise he made no comment.

"So that's it," he said at last. He sighed. "Well, I had to know. But I hoped it wasn't Clayton."

"Because of Denise?"

"Because of Denise. If I have to—expose her father, she will always believe it was a form of vengeance. Well, it can't be helped. Freelton will be here any day, and when he comes there is bound to be a showdown. It won't be pleasant. You understand that, don't you?"

"Yes, I understand. But it has to be done, as you say. Oh, Peter, why do people have to be so greedy?"

"God knows," he said heavily.

From the open windows of the gameroom came the sound of Benny Goodman's band.

"You must go back before you are missed," he said regretfully.

"Yes," she agreed. She did not move.

His arms went around her, holding her so closely that she could feel the drumming of his heart under her cheek. His lips moved over her hair. Then he let her go.

She turned without a backward look and went around the lilac hedge onto the terrace. In the darkness something moved. Dan Holt got out of a garden chair.

"That was the chauffeur, wasn't it?" he asked curtly.

Jill raised her eyebrows. She did not answer.

"The fortune hunter," Dan said. "Are you crazy, to be meeting a guy like that?"

"Dan, where are you going?" she asked in alarm.

"I'm going to have a word with that fellow."

Jill flung out a hand to stop him, but Dan had already disappeared in the darkness. She wanted to run after him, to stop him. She made herself stay where she was. Peter could take care of himself. She had better not interfere. She went back into the gameroom, where she was promptly claimed by an impatient partner and swept across the floor.

It was nearly half an hour before Dan returned. Jill had danced and laughed and bantered, but her eyes kept returning anxiously to the French windows. It was hard to keep her mind on what was said.

What was happening out on the lawn in the dark? What were Dan Holt and Peter Carr saying to each other? Were they fighting?

She had just laughingly refused a gin and tonic and demanded her usual lemonade when Dan appeared at her side. She looked at him quickly. He was unruffled. She sighed with relief. At least, they had not been fighting.

"What on earth have you been doing all this time?" she asked eagerly.

"Talking," Dan replied. "Very interesting. He's quite a guy." There was an odd expression on Dan Holt's face. "Quite a guy."

XXI

Two days later, the alarm clock jangled and Jill sat up, startled by the unexpected and discordant sound. Six o'clock. Why on earth had she wanted to be awakened so early? Oh, of course, this was the morning when she was going to New York. She had made the plan the afternoon before in the office of the Mapleville *Gazette*.

"The best man," Loomis had said, "is Hector Masters, who has become an authority on civic betterment. But I doubt if he'll be interested in such small potatoes as the village of Mapleville, Connecticut. Anyhow, it's such short notice he'll undoubtedly have other plans."

"Why shouldn't he be interested?" Jill demanded. "Every single citizen counts, Mr. Loomis."

He laughed. "Masters is in New York. I'll

get him on the telephone and let you talk to him. Maybe he will be willing to see you, at any rate."

Hector Masters had declared that he would be delighted to see Miss Bellamy in his New York office at eleven o'clock the following morning. It was weeks since she had been in New York, and she had decided to stay over-night at the Gotham, where she was well known, do some shopping, and perhaps see a play.

Before Jill left, she looked in on Mr. Bennett, propped up in bed.

"And what are you up to next, young lady?"

She told him about her New York inter-view with Hector Masters for the following day.

"New York? That will be good for you. Nice to have a change. Look here, Gillian, could you do a small errand for me while you're in the big city?"

"I'd love to," she assured him.

"All right. I want to send a message to my old gallery. Would you mind delivering it? Here it is. But not a word," he warned her. "I'm not supposed to be working. They've put the old man on the shelf temporarily, and Maud approves. Don't say anything to Maud

— or to Chester,eh?"

"Cross my heart," she promised.

It was a magnificent day, sparkling and bright, with a deep blue sky in which puffy white clouds floated. Jill opened the garage doors, checked on her suitcase, started the car, and rolled out of the garage. She put her foot on the brake.

"Lady, kin I thumb a ride?"

Peter Carr, in a beautifully cut linen suit, a suitcase at his feet, stood beside the driveway, his thumb raised, looking at her with the smile that made her heart turn over.

Her face lit up with pleasure and then was shadowed with disappointment.

"Good morning, Peter. Oh, I'm sorry. I'd love to give you a lift but I'm driving to New York."

"And I was hoping to be driven to New York," he said. "Coincidence, isn't it?"

"Oh, wonderful!" Darn, why did she always have to betray her feelings? She moved across the seat so that he could take the wheel. "How did you know I was going?"

"You told Denise when you were swimming yesterday, and Dan Holt reported to me."

He drove competently, his hands light and sure on the wheel, his eyes on the road. Jill stole a look at him. This morning he was even better-looking than she had remembered, and there was something different about him. A new light in his eyes when he looked at her, a demanding light, a confident light.

There was a long silence between them, but it was a silence without awkwardness. Then she said, "Peter?"

"Madam?"

"Dan Holt 'reported' to you that I was going to New York?"

"He did indeed."

"What—what happened when he followed you the other night?"

"We talked," he said laconically.

"Oh, must you be so mysterious? At first I was afraid—that is, I thought—"

Jim grinned. "That we were going to beat each other up? Not at all. Very civilized and polite. He's quite a guy."

"That's what he said about you."

Jim's grin deepened.

"Oh, I could shake you! What happened?"

He laughed outright at her exasperation. "Lady, weren't you ever taught to control your curiosity?" he teased her. "Consider the tragic fate of the curious cat."

"I—could—hit—you."

"All right. *Kamerad*. I surrender. I talk.

261

Holt's a nice guy. I had a hunch I could trust him, so I told him what I suspected was going on, at least so far as it concerns you and your safety. Sometimes it's a good idea to have a few reserves to draw on, someone on your side. And anyhow, I can't keep an eye on you all the time. He'll take over when I'm not around. Watchdog, bodyguard, or what have you."

"I don't need a bodyguard."

"Don't you?" he said in his quiet voice.

Somehow the gaiety went out of the summer morning. "Peter—what did you mean about locking my door?"

He answered the alarm in her voice. "Just a precaution," he said lightly. "Probably not in the least necessary, but it can't do any harm. Anyhow, it won't be long now."

"Oh." After a pause she asked, "Are you sure?"

"Almost." He concentrated on passing a car and said casually, "I told you it was an interesting talk. Holt told me that Denise is wrong. You aren't engaged to marry Chester Bennett."

"Of course I'm not," Jill said indignantly. "I'm not engaged to anyone." Darn, she thought, I shouldn't have said that as though —as though I thought he'd care. "I don't see

262

how that came into the conversation."

"Don't you?" Jim's laughing eyes met hers with a light in them that made her heart beat faster. "Holt also said—let the best man win."

"Oh." For the life of her Jill couldn't have added another word.

"Where are you staying?" Jim asked, his voice impersonal again.

"The Gotham. I've always stayed there when I was in New York. How about you?"

"I'll go to my apartment. I want to pick up some things, anyhow. Did you often stay at the Gotham with your father?"

"Several times. We lived abroad mostly, you know."

"Do you remember your mother, Jill?" he asked abruptly.

She shook her head. "How many people have asked me that lately! No, I don't remember her clearly. I was only four when— when I lost her."

"Sorry. I didn't mean to hurt you," he said contritely.

His gentle tone brought tears stinging her eyes. She blinked them away. "It doesn't hurt anymore. At least—not often."

"What are you planning to do in the city?"

Jill told him about her appointment with

Hector Masters. Beyond that there was nothing special. Some shopping. Perhaps a theater. "Oh, I nearly forgot. I promised Mr. Bennett to deliver a note for him to the man who took over his gallery when he retired. Darn. Oh, well, that shouldn't take long."

"Would you like me to deliver it for you?" he asked quickly.

"Wouldn't it be a nuisance?"

"Not at all," he answered truthfully. "Where is this place?"

Jill opened her handbag and read the address: *Oliver Noonan, Contemporary Art Groups, 57th Street.*

"Look here," Jim said. "You see this perfect day I arranged for you? Will you make it perfect for me? Dine and do a theater and dance a little? I've never danced with you, Jill. There's so much we haven't shared —yet."

Again there was that new confident note in his voice. Because Dan Holt had said she was not engaged? Dan had said, "Let the best man win." But what had Peter Carr told him?

"You will dine with me? Please," he implored her.

"I'd like to."

"Thank you. The Gotham at seven?"

He left her at the Gotham and arranged to

park her car at the Coliseum Garage. When Jill had booked a room and left her suitcase, she hailed a taxi and went to keep her appointment with Hector Masters. She found him in an unexpectedly impressive suite of offices on Fifth Avenue — a tall, thin, bespectacled man with the absent look of a scholar and the resonant voice and perfect diction of the professional speaker.

If he was surprised by her youth he gave no indication of it, and he listened with interest to what she had to say. When she had finished, she looked at him anxiously.

He smiled. "You are a good salesman, Miss Bellamy." He pulled his desk calendar toward him, consulted it, made a note. "There! The Bellamy Institute of Art, Mapleville, Connecticut, July the Fourth at eight p.m."

XXII

New York was hot. Sweltering. Like a wet blanket that smothered her. Like a Turkish bath. People walked slowly, men carrying their jackets, women wearing as little clothing as they dared, keeping in the shade as far as possible. Taxis darted in and out of line, creeping into the narrowest possible space and adding to the gasoline fumes that made the heavy air even harder to breathe.

Even so, the windows of the Fifth Avenue shops fascinated Jill as they always did. She stopped to look at a necklace of perfectly matched pearls at Tiffany's, to peer through the window at Steuben's to see the exquisite glass arranged against dark velvet, to examine amusing beach clothes and nightgowns with matching robes as delicate as cobwebs.

She ate a light lunch of fruit salad, hot rolls and iced coffee in an air-cooled restaurant.

266

She lingered over the meal, reluctant to face the hot blast of air, the relentless sun on the blistering pavements. The light reflecting from steel and glass buildings had almost blinded her with its fierce glare and she had left her dark glasses in the car pocket. She certainly wasn't going to do any shopping. Not in a New York heat wave.

What then? Go back to her hotel room and rest in preparation for the evening? The evening with Peter Carr! Her heart sang at the prospect. But she hated to waste a whole afternoon In New York. An air-cooled movie? That would pass a lot of time.

The decision came almost without her knowing how she had arrived at it. She had been letting Peter Carr shoulder her problems for her. She wasn't doing anything about them herself. Was there anything she could do?

The missing pages of the catalogue! Her father had worked on it with the help of his faithful secretary, Miss Pritchard, who had worked for him as long as Jill could remember. A slim, alert woman without any family of her own, who loved art and liked the stimulus of foreign travel. She had accompanied them on their wanderings across Europe and had returned to America when

Thomas Bellamy died. He had left her an ample pension and she had settled in New York, where she did occasional editorial work on art books.

Jill looked for a telephone and dialed the number. A familiar voice answered, rose in delight when she recognized her caller. Jill was to come at once.

Miss Pritchard lived in an old remodeled brownstone on Murray Hill. She flung open the door, both hands extended, drew Jill in and kissed her warmly.

"Heavens!" she exclaimed. "You've turned into a beauty. It's incredible."

Jill laughed outright and the older woman joined in, amused by her own awkward speech.

"Tactlessly put," she admitted. "I didn't mean it like that."

She had changed very little in three years. A well-bred woman with a flair for clothes and what Thomas Bellamy had called "a hospitable mind." Her eager curiosity and warm responsiveness made traveling with her an unending delight. She was never bored, never complained, never lost her fresh interest in the new and strange.

There was a touch of gray in her dark hair now which only added to her distinction. She wore a dress of thin white linen with a narrow black belt. Her hair was swept up from a thin, clever face that was interesting without being pretty.

Her living room, high-ceilinged with long windows, was a gracious place, with cream-colored summer slipcovers over couches and chairs, and wide bowls of red roses lending color to the pale room. The apartment was cool and restful and quiet. Above the white fireplace there was a Manet seascape, a water color which Jill recognized. Her father had bequeathed it to his secretary.

Miss Pritchard followed Jill's eyes. "Remember it? I always loved that scene. How like your father to think of the joy it would give me. Now let me really see you. Yes, you're lovely. So like your mother. Yet so unlike her. And you probably have her quality of eternal youth. When I saw her last winter she didn't look more than thirty."

Her voice rose sharply. "What's the matter, dear? The heat? Sit down. Put your head—"

"You saw my mother—last winter?" Jill said slowly. "Only a few months ago?"

"Why, yes. I had a stubborn attack of bronchitis in January, so I just dropped everything and went over to the South of France. She—*what's wrong?*"

"I thought—I didn't know—she was still alive. I always understood she had died years ago."

"Good heavens!" Miss Pritchard was aghast. "Have I done something terrible?"

"No, of course not. Tell me, Miss Pritchard. Please tell me—all about her."

There was a troubled look on the clever face, an odd uncertainty in the woman whose crisp assurance had always made her a tower of strength.

"How much do you remember about your mother, my dear?"

"Only that she was pretty—and gay—and adventurous." Jill's throat tightened. "She went away. That's all I ever knew."

As Miss Pritchard watched her, Jill searched her memory. "Oh, I remember something more. She wanted the Bellamy jewel collection."

"Yes, she wanted things," Miss Pritchard said shortly. "Sari Bellamy wanted—everything. When you were only four years old, and such an adorable child, sweet and gay and affectionate, she divorced your father and married a man named Grierson, a Texas oil man, who had millions. Later she left him for an impoverished English baronet, who was considerably older than she was. By that

270

time she had more money than even she could spend, but she wanted what the Texan couldn't give her, titled society. She became Lady Compton. A few years ago the Englishman died, and she married a Frenchman years younger than she, because society was stodgy. The same old thing. No excitement in it, particularly with an elderly husband who was ultraconventional and bored by exploring the gay spots. She wanted Life with a capital L. She is now Comtesse de Mariot. Sari is still beautiful, still incredibly young, still dissatisfied, still seeking—" Miss Pritchard made a helpless gesture—"I don't know what. Neither does she. The pot of gold at the end of the rainbow, perhaps. I used to dislike her because she had left her child without regret, because she abandoned a husband who loved her. Loved her so deeply. But when I saw her last winter, I was—sorry. She has so much and she's so empty."

"Did she mention me?" Jill asked wistfully. "Or has she forgotten I ever existed?"

"She asked a lot about you. Showered me with questions. I showed her some snapshots I had of you at all ages and the picture of you that the Viennese photographer won a prize with. The white profile against a white background. Remember it? Like a cameo. She cried over it." Miss Pritchard fell silent.

Jill waited for a moment. Then she said steadily, "Go on, please. I'd rather know it all. It's always better to know, isn't it? Even when it hurts. My father taught me that."

There were tears in Miss Pritchard's eyes. "He loved you so much. After Sari disillusioned him, I think you were the only human being he ever truly loved."

"Go on about my mother, please."

"Well, Sari cried when she saw that picture, but not because she had walked out on a lovely daughter. She cried because you are prettier than she ever was. Because you are younger. Because you may marry and have children."

"But why shouldn't I?" Jill cried in rebellion.

"Because then Sari, the glamorous but aging wife of a young husband, would be a grandmother," Miss Pritchard said grimly, "and she can't face it."

"Well," Jill said flatly, "at least I know."

"Now tell me what has been happening to you?" the older woman asked eagerly, glad to escape the painful subject.

Jill poured out the story of her accidents, of the mismanagement of the Institute, while her father's former secretary listened, white-faced.

At length, she said, "I never met any of the three governors, though I do remember that your father took a long time selecting them. But I do know this. Thomas Bellamy knew more about art and less about people than anyone I ever encountered. He made few mistakes about paintings and lots of mistakes about men and women."

She considered for a moment. "But there's one sure thing. I have—now where did I see it? My safety deposit box? My old files in the basement? I came across it just the other day. But where—where? Oh, of course!"

She went swiftly into the foyer and knelt before a low bookcase, pulled a thick leather-bound volume from the bottom shelf, and opened it on the desk between the two long windows that faced the street. It was a filing case. She turned over papers impatiently, drew out a packet of long blue sheets stapled together.

"The catalogue!" Jill cried in excitement. "I thought you might have a copy!"

Together, the two women pored over it. Jill was the first to discover the mention of the Praxiteles bust. Miss Pritchard found the Picasso and the Matisse, which had been in the box Peter Carr had found at Penn Manor.

"Take it with you," Miss Pritchard said. "No, wait. Before you do that, I'll make a typewritten copy for you to take, instead. I'll keep this copy in my safety deposit box. It may be needed as evidence. Your father's handwritten corrections and his initials are on every page. There could be no question about its authenticity."

"But it would take you hours to do that," Jill said doubtfully.

"I have hours," Miss Pritchard assured her. "And it's a small thing to do for Thomas. For Thomas's daughter. You're staying at the Gotham as usual, I suppose. I'll have a copy of the catalogue delivered there sometime before midnight. But my dear — be careful. Be very careful."

Jill turned for a final inspection in the full-length mirror. The coral dress was stunning, she thought. Like a cloud at sunset. She clasped the emerald bracelet on her left wrist, remembering again how her mother had wanted the Bellamy jewels.

Strange to think she had a mother, that the mother had been alive all these years. And not a word. Never a word.

For a moment Jill's throat tightened. Someday she would go to Europe and see the Comtesse de Mariot. Perhaps they could meet, and some spark would strike between them. Her mother might forgive her for having grown up. Perhaps she would even be a little fond of her.

Jill picked up a wrap and let herself out of her room. As she stepped out of the elevator she saw Peter. She had forgotten how tall he was. He was standing lost in thought. His evening clothes, as she remembered from the night at the inn, were superbly tailored. Every woman in the lobby had turned for a second look. But he was oblivious to the attention he was attracting, sunk in his thoughts. They must be serious thoughts. How grim he seemed.

Then, as though he felt her eyes upon him, he turned suddenly and smiled. Jill's heart soared. I love him, she thought. Whoever he is, whatever he is doing, I love him.

The restaurant he had chosen was cool and softly lighted, with deft silent service and superb food. He laughed at the enthusiasm with which she ordered and the gusto with which she ate. In fact, they both laughed a great deal over nothing at all, and talked as fast and hard as they could, both sense and

275

nonsense. It was as though they were suddenly in great haste to explore each other's minds, to reveal themselves.

They were so engrossed in each other that they did not observe the other diners, did not know how many eyes rested on them, looking first because they were so attractive a couple, and then returning with a smile because they were so much in love.

Jim had tickets for an excellent musical with an amusing book as well as lilting music. Afterwards they danced at a roof garden, with New York spread out below them, a fairyland of lights. Dancing with Peter Carr was unlike any other dancing she had ever done. She had known, of course, that he was a magnificent dancer. Following his firm lead, she found herself automatically doing new and intricate steps she had never tried before.

She looked up suddenly to see his eyes searching her face.

"What's wrong?" he asked in surprise.

"Nothing."

He grinned at her. "Oh, come off it! All of a sudden, you've grown chilly and withdrawn."

"I was just thinking I was sorry I can't tango as well as Miss Thompkins."

Jim's eyes glinted with humor. His heart sang. She was jealous of Lola. She must care about him at least a little.

"She is a superb dancer," he agreed. "By the way, she has left Mapleville for good." He smiled into her eyes. "There aren't many girls like you, who accept a man for what he is, without caring about what position he may occupy. Anyhow, dancing with her isn't the same thing as dancing with you. Nothing in the world is like dancing with you. I dreamed that it would be like this."

Suddenly Jill discovered that her feet had wings. She was dancing as well as Lola Thompkins. She wasn't jealous of the Spanish girl any more. She had no thoughts to spare for anyone but Peter. He shut out the world.

When they had returned to their table she asked, "Did you remember about delivering Mr. Bennett's note to his gallery?"

"Oh, yes, I took it to the gallery and turned it over to Mr. Noonan in person." Jim added thoughtfully, "Mr. Oliver Noonan."

"Is there any answer for me to take back?"

"Keep this under your hat, lady. For a few days, anyhow. Mr. Noonan is going to answer the letter in person. And I think he is going to provide quite a shock to quite a few people. Someone, at least, is going to wish he had never heard of Mr. Noonan. He is probably going to wish he had never been born."

Jill shivered. "I never knew you could look so—so hard, so relentless."

"Relentless! I'm thinking of gas turned on in a defenseless girl's room. Of brakes that had been tampered with on a helpless girl's car. Relentless? There are no words for what I feel."

"Which one is it, Peter?"

The level eyes were abstracted. For a moment they seemed hardly aware of her. "Noonan wouldn't tell me."

"But he knows about what has been going on at the Institute?"

"Some of it, yes. Once I broke down his—resistance, he talked quite a bit."

"I don't know what you are getting at. Do you have to be so mysterious?"

He laughed at her. "Your eyes snap so they look like twinkling stars. You're—you're so beautiful in that coral dress you take my breath away. I can't keep my mind on my great and dramatic story."

She flushed. "Well, try to. I'm dying to know the whole thing."

"Whatever you say, lady," he agreed with mock obedience. "It seems that Mr. Noonan took over Mr. Bennett's art dealership. He isn't handling such big-name painters but he has some promising newcomers. Noonan is a painter himself, but as he admits, derivative. Not much originality. But for years he has been earning a modest living by—guess what?"

Jill's eyes widened. "Copying pictures!"

"Go to the head of the class. Mr. Oliver Noonan is a tall man, rather untidy, with stormy eyes that are like gimlets. Remind you of anyone?"

"John Jones!" she cried in excitement. "Then, at least, Mr. Bennett is in the clear. Thank heaven for that. He'd never have sent me to Mr. Noonan, knowing I had seen John Jones."

He smiled at her. "It's been worrying you, hasn't it?"

"Not knowing. That's the worst. You can face things if you know what you've got to face."

Jim paid the check and followed Jill out of the room, noticing the regal carriage of the small proud head, the grace of the coral-clad figure.

"It's still my evening," he declared when they reached the warm street, "and we are going to forget the governors and the Institute until tomorrow."

He beckoned to a taxi, drove to the garage where he had left Jill's car. They rode for hours, across the Triborough Bridge and out Long Island; returned to cross the George Washington Bridge and look back at the lights of the city. She told him about her successful interview with Hector Masters and then about finding a copy of her father's catalogue in the possession of his former secretary.

"There will be a copy waiting for me at the Gotham tonight."

"That's wonderful news. Now we'll have the kind of evidence we need."

"Peter!"

"Yes, my beauti—yes, Jill?"

"How did you persuade Mr. Noonan to come up to Mapleville? He's deeply involved, isn't he?"

"Deeply," he agreed. "Right up to his neck."

"Then?"

"I made an agreement with him. I'll tell you later, because I'm sure you'll approve. It's all right. Trust me."

"I do," she said quietly. After a long pause she said, "I've been thinking. If Oliver Noonan is John Jones, it should logically be Mr. Bennett who is involved, and yet he's the one I'm surest is in the clear. When someone threw rocks at me, he and Mr. Allen were together at the Institute. When I was locked in the warehouse, he was with Mr. Clayton. But—that means they all have alibis! It couldn't be any one of the governors."

There was a silence. After a long time she forced herself to ask, "Is it Chester? That would explain so much. And yet I can't bear it."

He put his hand on hers. "We'll know soon enough. Try not to worry."

He parked the car and they took the ferry to Staten Island, looked down at the dark water, ate peanuts and drank orange juice. On the ferry coming back, they watched the lights of Manhattan blink out, one by one. The last of the cleaning women's lights went out in the high buildings, the street lights went out. Then the water was a path of gold from the rising sun.

"Good lord," he said, contrite. "I've kept you up all night! I ought to be shot. You'll be exhausted, much too tired to drive back today."

"I'm not tired at all," she said, her eyes shining. "I'm wide awake. Let's change and have breakfast and drive home this morning while it's still cool."

"Sure?"

"I'm sure."

There was no one on the upper deck of the shabby ferry plowing its staid way like a tired old woman across the river. Inside, they could see a dozing guard. They were alone with the dawn.

"A new day. Another wonderful day," Jill said.

Jim took her in his arms, kissed her hair and her lips, her eyes and her lips, her lips.

"A new day," he said.

XXIII

"If you're going to change for dinner, you had better get a move on," Mrs. Meam said. "Not that your pink-and-white gingham isn't cute as a button. You look about fourteen in it. But it's no way to dress for a dinner party."

"I still have an hour." Jill closed the oven door, her cheeks pink with heat and exertion. "Plenty of time."

"Seems like you ought to rest a bit before you play hostess. You've been working on this dinner for hours. But I'll say this child. You know things about cooking I never taught you. How did you do it?"

"I've studied all the gourmet cookbooks I could find. Talk about homework! Do you really think it's a good dinner?"

"The best I ever heard of. Now run along and rest."

"First, I want to make a final check, be

sure everything is all right. Oh, where are the glasses, do you know?"

"I was housekeeper here for Andrew Trevor," Mrs. Meam said dryly. "I know this house like I do my own. That cupboard over there. Good crystal. What possessed you, giving a dinner here?"

"I don't know. I loved the house the minute I saw it. I want to buy it and live in it as soon as I come of age. It's for sale, you know."

"Yes." Mrs. Meam was troubled. "I guess Mr. Trevor needs the money right bad. Miss Thompkins told me before she left. Seems she knew the Trevors, father and son, out West. Mr. Trevor must of come down a long way. He's just a roustabout on the oilfields, she said. Not a penny to bless himself with."

"Poor man! At least I'd take good care of his house. Make it come alive again. Aunt Sally, as soon as dinner is over, have the maids clear up quickly and then all of you leave here as soon as you can."

"You up to something, child?"

"Just—just a game. Now," she added quickly, "I'll see to the flowers and place cards and then change."

"What are you going to wear?"

"That sapphire crepe. Now what was I

—oh, the flowers."

She inspected the long table in the dining room at Penn Manor. Tonight, with lights blazing, the gracious house had come to life. She looked at the place cards. Everyone had accepted. Even the Bennetts were coming, the doctor having given his grudging consent, provided that Mr. Bennett left early. She counted on her fingers: the Bennetts and Chester; Roger Clayton, Denise and Dan Holt; Abraham Allen; Miss Pritchard, who had listened to a breathless telephone call and promptly accepted; and an extra girl, Sally Curtis, to keep the table setting even.

Jill had planned and cooked most of the dinner herself. Mrs. Meam would handle the kitchen and the Bennett maids were to serve.

In a guest bedroom upstairs Jill dressed in the sapphire crepe with its swirling skirt and matching slippers. The color had seemed becoming when she bought it, but tonight Jill felt that her eyes looked too large, her face was too pale now that the flush from cooking had died out. Try as she would, she could not forget that somewhere in the attic were the boxes that had been taken from the warehouse, that someone at the dinner party was desperately anxious to retrieve them.

Dan Holt, she knew, had been keeping an

unobtrusive eye on the house all day, and to-night, while he was a dinner guest, Peter Carr would replace him on guard duty.

What was going to happen tonight? Her heart thudded with suspense and anxiety. It seemed to her that now the time had come, she did not want to know the truth.

At the last moment, she had telephoned her guests to explain that the dinner party was to be held at Penn Manor. There had been practically no opportunity for anyone to try to remove the boxes so far. But tonight?

"Give him whatever chance he needs," Peter Carr had advised her. "Sometime during the evening start a game of hide and seek. At a certain time give each of them a flashlight. Then put out the lights. One of them is to hide and the rest are to hunt him through the house by flashlight. Clear?"

It was clear. It was a good plan—if it worked. Undoubtedly the one who had hidden the boxes would want to be the one to hide, to take advantage of the darkness and confusion in the unfamiliar house to remove them from the basement.

Jill was frightened. Now, at the last minute when it was too late to change her plans, she wanted to say, "Let's let it go. I don't want to know."

She ran down the stairs as the doorbell rang. Abraham Allen was the first of her guests to arrive. He gave her a sour smile.

"Are you trying to convince me by this stunt that Penn Manor is a good buy?" he asked.

"I'm hoping the house will convince you without my help," she said with a forced smile. *Is he the one?* she wondered. Is that why he is so early? So he'll have time to reconnoiter?

Miss Pritchard, stunning in a long black dress with a white lace jacket, was next. Her keen eyes brushed Jill's face. She whispered, "Chin up, my dear! You can take it," and turned graciously toward Abraham Allen when Jill introduced him.

"The town benefactor," she said, holding out her hand. "I have heard so much of your work. This is a very great pleasure."

Jill smothered a giggle. For a moment Abraham Allen's dour expression was gone. He almost beamed. How the man longed for popularity and approval!

The Bennetts came next, and then Chester, who was dutifully escorting Sally Curtis. Mr. Bennett seemed to have recovered completely. His ruddy color was restored.

"Well," he chuckled, "here I am with bells

on, and my mouth watering. If the dinner isn't good I've a horrible punishment in mind for you. I want fo-o-od." He dragged out the word.

"Wait until you taste it," Jill boasted. "The order of the *cordon bleu* will admit me. This meal is the masterpiece on which I intend to rest my fame."

"As long as there's plenty. I've been starved for days and it seems like years."

Is he the one? Jill thought. This kindly cheerful man?

Mrs. Bennett, in a dark green evening dress that made her look more sallow than ever, gave Jill a nervous look.

"Such a strange idea," she complained. "Dining in a deserted house. Really, Gillian, you get more peculiar every day."

"It's a thrilling idea," Sally exclaimed. "I've always been crazy to see this place. Can we explore, Gillian? Please say yes. I'm dying to go over it."

"Later," Jill promised her.

"Every nook and corner?"

"Every nook and corner."

Roger Clayton and Denise arrived with Dan Holt. Clayton kissed Jill's cheek.

"Is that all right?" he asked in his big voice. "Okay to kiss the chef?"

"Obligatory," she laughed. *Was he the one?*

"Now that's good news." Dan Holt kissed her cheek lightly, whispered, "Okay. Carr is taking over at the back of the house. He'll keep an eye on that basement door." Aloud he said, "Sapphire is your color. It's terrific. In fact, you're terrific."

Denise laughed. "But a bit out of character with your new role, isn't it, Gillian?" she asked sweetly. "A cap and apron would be more appropriate."

When she had introduced Miss Pritchard as an old friend, the latter studied them with swift, scrutinizing glances. In New York, Jill had sketched their main characteristics as well as she could. Miss Pritchard recognized the traits Jill had mentioned. What a pity, she thought, that Thomas Bellamy had lacked his daughter's instinctive knowledge of human beings.

The dinner was all that Jill had promised, from the soup of crab with sherry to the chocolate soufflé. Now and then, Mrs. Meam stole out of the kitchen into the darkened smaller dining room to listen to the words of praise and delight, her face beaming with pride. Jill was flushed with pleasure. She almost forgot the purpose of this dinner party, the trap that was baited. The trap that was to be sprung by someone at this table.

At last, Bennett said with a sigh of repletion, "My dear, you could make a fortune by cooking. A gourmet meal from start to finish."

"Gillian doesn't need to make a fortune," Denise commented. "Do you, dear?"

"Still," Jill countered lightly, "it's nice to know I don't have to depend on one."

"I do hope you won't have indigestion, William," his wife said anxiously. "You ate too much."

They moved into the great drawing room for coffee. Afterwards, Sally reminded Jill of her promise to show them the house. It seemed to Jill that there was a stirring of unrest in the room. Someone was afraid, so afraid that the fear, like a tangible thing, troubled the air.

"You're going to have to do it on your own," she declared, trying to speak gaily. She handed each of them a flashlight. "One of you is to hide, and when the lights go out the rest are to start searching. Use your flashlights. The finder will get a prize. Who wants to hide?"

Her heart pounded. She could hardly

breathe. Which of her guests would grasp this opportunity?

"Let me, Gillian," Denise said. "Please! Let me."

Jill caught her breath. Denise? It couldn't be possible. Something had gone wrong with Peter's plan.

"Of course," she said steadily. She reached for the light switch. "I'll give you five minutes to find your hiding place. When the clock strikes nine we will start hunting." She pressed the switch and the room was dark.

There was a tapping of high heels as Denise ran out of the room. Then silence. She must have stopped to take off her slippers. Someone moved quietly in the room.

"Don't begin yet," Jill called warningly. "Everyone is to start at once."

The clock struck the hour and the flashlights went on, moving like darting fireflies. In a few minutes the party had scattered, some of them going back to the library and up the circular staircase, others up the front stairs.

"William," Mrs. Bennett cried, "the doctor won't like it if you overexert."

He chuckled. "I was just figuring what I'd do if I were hiding. I'd go outside, wait for the drawing room to be clear and then slip in behind the curtains of that open window. I'm going to sit right here and catch the bird without moving."

Jill listened to the movements through the house, running feet, people bumping into each other, laughter, exclamations. She went swiftly through the dining rooms and into the kitchen. As they had been instructed, Mrs. Meam and the maids had gone.

For a moment she switched out her light and stood in the darkness. Then she opened the back door and went out quietly. Somewhere in the night Peter would be waiting. Waiting for someone to enter the basement and try to retrieve the boxes.

Not a sound. A movement? No, just the rustling of leaves. A whisper? Was it Peter? Through the windows she could see the flashlights moving from room to room, hear startled exclamations and laughter, hear Sally exclaiming shrilly, "Isn't this thrilling?"

A movement. A gasp. She switched on her light. Caught in its beam were a man with a woman in his arms. The woman was Denise, in a chiffon dress of pale yellow. The man who looked into the light, his eyes wide and startled, was Peter Carr.

Jill switched off the light, felt blindly for the doorknob, re-entered the house. I'm going to be sick, she thought. She took a long breath. She couldn't think. Her mind was a whirling chaos.

Somewhere in the darkness near her there was the ghost of a sound, not a footstep. It was the almost undetectable sound of cloth brushing against cloth. Jill snapped to alertness. She froze against the door, hardly daring to breathe.

Someone in the kitchen took a quick gasping breath and was silent again. And behind her, the doorknob moved noiselessly under her hand. Someone trying to get in. Peter? Denise?

She stepped out of her slippers, moved to one side. A shrouded light flashed on the kitchen floor, found the basement door, and went out again. Behind the light she had seen nothing but a black shadow. She was pressed against the wall now, lips parted so she could breathe silently.

The back door was opening slowly, an inch at a time, without any noise. She was aware of it only when she felt the cool night air on her ankles.

The prowler had reached the basement door, opened it. The light flashed for a moment on the stairs and went out. In a moment the door had closed again. Under it there was a thread of light. The flash must seem safe to use now.

Jill was aware that someone stood beside her in the kitchen. Close enough to touch. It was Peter. She was sure of it without knowing how she knew. She remained still. From the basement came a sound, a window being pushed up. Something grated.

Then the silent figure beside her moved swiftly, going straight to the basement door. Flung it open. Jill pressed behind him. The light in the basement went out and there was a startled exclamation.

A long finger of light reached down the stairs, crawled over the furnace, moved toward the window, found the stooping figure searching wildly around the big basement, and caught the white face in a noose of light.

Chester Bennett!

Jill never forgot that moment. All her life there would be nights when she would dream of Chester, trapped in that noose of light, turning to them a face like death.

He straightened up, and came to meet them, staggering like a drunken man. The flashlight was switched off and Peter Carr reached up to turn on the basement lights.

Then, without moving, he said quietly, "The boxes aren't here, Bennett. I moved them the other day. I put them in a safer place."

"Boxes?" Chester tried to look puzzled, tried to pull himself together. "I don't know what you're talking about, Carr. We're playing a game, hunting in the dark for Denise Clayton. Miss Bellamy's game."

"You've been playing my game and it's up, Bennett."

Chester ran his tongue over his dry lips. "What—what do you think I'm up to?"

There was no hardness, no relentlessness, in Peter's face now, Jill thought. Instead, there was sadness and a profound pity.

"I think you're looking for the boxes you cached here. The boxes you took out of the warehouse before you set the place on fire."

Not Chester. I can't bear it to be Chester. Not Chester.

"Didn't you, Bennett?" Peter asked, his voice insistent.

"Yes," Chester said at last, dully. "I set fire to the warehouse." His voice broke. "But I swear to God, Carr, I never meant you to burn. I—I did my best to save you."

"I know you did," Peter's voice was still gentle, still profoundly sad, it seemed to Jill. There was no triumph in his manner. "Well," he said at last, "we mustn't spoil Miss Bellamy's dinner party."

Chester was bewildered. "What—what do you mean?"

"For you to go back and help finish the game."

"And then what?"

"Why, go on home, of course." There was a faint touch of surprise in the other man's voice.

"You aren't going to—do anything about it?" Chester sounded incredulous.

The silence was longer. "Not tonight, at any rate." Peter turned to Jill. "Go on with your party, Miss Bellamy. Nothing more will happen tonight." He turned quickly and went out of the basement. Swift sure footsteps sounded across the kitchen floor. He left the house.

Jill waited at the top of the stairs for Chester, who came up slowly, as though he were very tired or very old. They did not look at each other. Without a word he accompanied her back to the drawing room. The lights had gone on and for a moment they stood blinking in the brilliant glare. They were met by a burst of triumphant laughter.

William Bennett was holding Denise by the

arm. "You see," he crowed. "I just sat still and waited and she climbed in the window and ran right into my arms. They also catch who only sit and wait." He raised his clasped hands over his head. "The winnah! And still champeen! Prize, please."

Jill joined in the laughter and applause and presented him with a cigarette case in which a watch was set. He made a grandiloquent speech of acceptance, followed by cheers, and then added: "I'm out on parole from my doctor. I'm due back home, like Cinderella, but at ten-thirty instead of midnight. Sorry to spoil the party."

Jill saw the Bennetts drive away. Abraham Allen, at his own suggestion, escorted Miss Pritchard, who was going to the inn. Dan took Sally, while Roger Clayton and Denise drove off with a graven-faced Peter Carr at the wheel.

They were all gone now but Chester Bennett. "Will you drive me home?" Jill asked him.

They rode in silence. They had reached the Bennett house before Jill said brokenly, "I'd have given you the money if you needed it. Did you have to try to kill me, Chester?"

He drove the car into the garage, set the brake, and dropped his head on his folded arms on the wheel.

"I did what — I had to do. Go away, Jill. Leave me alone. For God's sake, leave me alone."

XXIV

The meeting had been called in the director's room for ten o'clock, the morning after Jill's dinner party at Penn Manor. This was Peter Carr's plan and Jill had followed it blindly, making the arrangements as soon as she had returned from New York.

She could not bear to remember that day, that perfect day, and the night which had culminated on the ferry in Peter's arms, with Peter's mouth covering her own, warm and gentle yet demanding. Twenty-four hours later, he had held Denise Clayton in his arms. Only twenty-four hours!

In a simple white cotton dress with a full skirt and round neck, she looked incredibly young for the role she was to play. And the person she would have to expose publicly was Chester Bennett. It seemed to her that she could not do it. Even Peter, who had felt such deadly anger, had showed only gentleness and compassion in dealing with him.

Then she remembered. Her heart hardened. Such a man had no right to be free. No one would be safe while he was left at liberty to act.

There was another intolerable problem to face—how much the Bennetts would suffer when they knew the truth. Or had Mr. Bennett suspected the truth? That would account for the unexpectedly violent quarrel between father and son. She winced as she thought that they would accuse her of ingratitude.

As soon as breakfast was over, she got out her car and drove to the Institute. Miss Pritchard, as usual in smart black and white, a tiny hat tilted over her clever, narrow face, was there ahead of her. She held the long blue pages of the catalogue and she was moving from item to item, checking them off the list.

She welcomed Jill with a smile, which faded when she had studied the girl's face with loving eyes.

"What's wrong, my dear? You look like a ghost. Didn't it work out according to plan last night?"

"It was Chester Bennett." Jill framed the words soundlessly with numb lips.

"Oh, you poor child! What a shock for

you. But we've got to see the thing through, you know. I need your help. I can check the collection against the catalogue. But I haven't your training or your eye. I can't detect copies, if there are any here. I'll leave that to you. When is the meeting to be?"

"Ten o'clock. We have nearly an hour."

Miss Pritchard laughed, trying to help Jill release her tension. "You should have been here when I arrived. Joe Deakam did everything but roll out the red carpet."

The outer door banged and Abraham Allen came in. His mouth tightened when he saw Jill.

"What on earth are you doing here now?" he asked.

"Looking for substitutions," she told him bluntly. She told him about the boxes that had been hidden in the warehouse and what they had been found to contain.

"This is preposterous, Miss Bellamy. You're setting the whole place by the ears with your grotesque imagination."

"It's not imagination," she retorted.

"Do you remember your mother?" he asked nastily.

"Why, no," she said, taken aback.

"What do you mean?" Miss Pritchard put in. She eyed Allen steadily. "Gillian naturally does not remember her mother. But I remember Sari Bellamy very well indeed. In fact, I saw her less than six months ago."

"She's in a mental institution, isn't she?"

The two women stared at him, wide-eyed. Jill was the first to recover.

"So that's it!" she said, enlightened. "You thought — all of you thought — the reason my mother had gone away was because she was insane. Now I understand. That explains the odd things Mrs. Bennett keeps saying to me, the way she seems almost to be afraid of me at times." She turned in appeal to Miss Pritchard.

"I can't imagine, Mr. Allen," the older woman said, "where you heard such unfounded and vicious nonsense. Gillian's mother left Mr. Bellamy. That's the whole sad story. She has married three times since then. She is now Comtesse de Mariot and she spends much of her time in the South of France. I might point out that she is as sane as anyone I know."

There was a little pause. "I am surprised," Miss Pritchard went on, "that a level-headed man like you would not be careful to verify the facts before accepting any such rumor."

"Sane!" Allen sat down heavily on the

stone bench against the wall. At length he looked up, his thin mouth twitching. "I owe you a profound apology, Miss Bellamy. Not that I was the only one to be misled. Clayton and Bennett both understood that there was hereditary madness in your family. I am — sorry. It seems inadequate. But then —" his face whitened — "then there is truth in the story about the Bellamy collection being raided, items stolen, copied, I don't know what . . ."

"It is true."

"But what happened to the originals?"

"Probably sold. We can't be sure yet."

"This means public exposure. Disgrace," Allen said. "It isn't fair that I should be involved in it. I've worked for this town. I have an honorable record. I wanted to be State Senator. Now that's over." He got up to pace the room. "Who found the boxes?"

"Peter Carr."

"Where?"

"In the basement at Penn Manor."

Allen's eyes narrowed. "I should have known," he said in relief. "He's a crook like his father. That's the real answer."

A car door slammed and Clayton came in with Bennett. They were laughing over some joke.

"We're all ahead of time," Clayton said, consulting his watch. "I still don't know who called this meeting or why we are here, but let's get started. It's a fine day for golf."

"I called the meeting," Jill said.

"You!" Bennett exclaimed in surpsise. "Well, after that dinner last night I guess we owe you a meeting. Shall we get on with it?"

"We're not all here yet."

"But — who else?"

The door opened again and Peter Carr came in with a white-faced Chester Bennett.

"Shall we go in now?" Jill asked. "Joe, bring two more chairs, will you?"

"Four more," Peter Carr corrected.

Clayton turned sharply to stare at his chauffeur, alerted by his tone.

"You've worked it out," he said. It was not a question.

"I've worked it out."

"Good work, Carr!"

There was a faint smile on his chauffeur's lips. "I think the business of Peter Carr is played out, sir."

"So do I," Allen snapped. "This fellow is James Trevor, son of Andrew Trevor, who left this town under a cloud four years ago."

Peter Carr was Andrew Trevor's son James! The world whirled about Jill. Steadied. *Crazy mad about Denise . . . A roustabout in the oil fields . . . Half the people in town lost their savings . . . A crook like his father.*

"Suppose," Jim Trevor said levelly, "we get on with the meeting. The problem of my father will be cleared up later, Honest Abe. Make no mistake about that."

Jill led the way, white-faced, shaking, her head held proudly high, to the director's room. She did not look at the man called Jim Trevor.

Without a word, he pulled out the chair at the head of the table for her and she sat down. The others took their seats. Chester looked like death. Jim was grim and silent. They were all surprised when Miss Pritchard joined them and laid on the table before her the blue pages of the Bellamy catalogue.

"Suppose," Jim said, "you open the meeting, Miss Bellamy."

She looked up, saw Clayton's alert eyes, Bennett's puzzled expression, which was gradually changing to alarm. Her throat closed. All along he must have guessed. That was the reason for the growing tension between him and Chester.

She looked at Peter—at Jim Trevor, she reminded herself—met the steady gray eyes. A great load was lifted off her heart. She made a little pleading gesture toward him.

"Please," she said. "I—can't."

"Of course, Miss Bellamy." Jim looked at his watch. "While we're waiting—"

"I was wondering who those other two chairs were for," Allen said. "If you have called strangers in here without authorization—"

"Let them speak for themselves when they come," Jim replied. He leaned back in his chair, relaxed and at ease. "I first heard of the Bellamy Institute of Art when I was called in by the head of my law firm, Mr. Garrison, of Garrison, Harper & Jennings."

Someone gasped.

"Mr. Garrison told me a queer story. One of the firm's clients, Miss Gillian Bellamy, claimed that three attempts had been made to —shall we say, injure her? He had learned this from Mr. Roger Clayton, who was one of the governors of the Institute. Mr. Garrison sent me up here to see if I could find out the truth. Only Mr. Clayton knew my identity."

Jill leaned forward, her hands clenched so tightly together they hurt her. Clayton was watchful, Allen grim, Bennett haggard. Chester sat with bent head, unmoving. Miss Pritchard was studying their faces with keen interest and the detachment that always distinguished her.

Jim looked again at his watch and suddenly Jill felt a thrill of horror. Something was going to happen. The net had closed on Chester Bennett. Perhaps he deserved it, but the pain was more than she could bear. She didn't want vengeance. She didn't want his father to suffer any more because of his son's actions.

Jim went on, tranquil, unhurried. He described his first encounter with Jill when she had been locked in the warehouse. He described the finding of the boxes with the identifying mark Φ. He told of returning to the warehouse, seeing the boxes removed, the useless attempt to break open the door of the locked room upstairs, and the setting of the fire which would destroy the evidence in the locked room. He had even found where the gasoline for the fire had come from.

He did not once look at Chester, but slowly Bennett's eyes turned to his son's stricken face, remained fixed on it.

Allen's expression was beginning to change. The look he gave Jim Trevor altered from hard suspicion to a kind of fear. Clayton had braced himself like a man prepared to spring into action.

Again Jim looked at his watch. "There was

one curious incident that puzzled me a lot. The man who Miss Bellamy believed had been using the warehouse for some unknown purpose, and who she believed threw the rocks which so nearly resulted in her drowning, was identified by Mrs. Sally Meam as her lodger, John Jones. Mr. Jones promptly disappeared. There was no word of him until I had an accidental encounter with him one night outside the Bennett garage, when he was having a secret meeting with—someone. He threw me into the Clayton swimming pool so I would not be able to identify him, and got away."

Again he looked at his watch. "But day before yesterday, Miss Bellamy kindly gave me a lift to New York, where I delivered a note for her to Mr. Oliver Noonan at the galleries which Mr. Bennett used to own. Mr. Noonan—"

The door of the director's room was flung open. A tall man stood there, a man with penetrating, stormy eyes and ill-tempered eyebrows.

"You talking about me?" he asked.

Jim waved him to one of the extra chairs. "This is Mr. Oliver Noonan," he said. "Better known in Mapleville as John Jones."

Noonan sat down with a defiant swagger.

"What have you been saying about me?"

"I hadn't started yet," Jim said mildly. "Mr. Noonan has been doing some work up here. In that locked room on the second floor of the warehouse he's been making copies of part of the Bellamy collection, some of them to sell, some of them to replace originals, which were sold."

Noonan half rose from his chair. "You gave me your word—"

"I said that if you would make a clear statement of your involvement and help return all the missing items, you would not be prosecuted."

"You've taken a lot on yourself, young man," Allen snapped. "I don't want any bad publicity for the Institute, but even so I am not willing to stand by and allow a criminal action to go unpunished."

"I represent Garrison, Harper & Jennings, which represents Miss Bellamy's interests," Jim said. "Miss Bellamy is not a vengeful person, for which you should all be profoundly grateful. The instructions from my firm have been for me to carry out Miss Bellamy's wishes in this very painful affair."

His eyes locked with hers for a moment in a question and an answer.

"All right?" he asked, as though no one

else were in the room.

"All right," she agreed.

Miss Pritchard looked swiftly from one face to the other. She smiled, enlightened.

"I want to make one thing clear," Noonan intervened. "I didn't bargain for what happened to the girl. I refused to have any part in it. That's why I cleared out of here."

"It was the newspaper article about the Praxiteles bust, The Man with the Broken Nose," Jim said, "that put me on the track. I got in touch with the Ohio collector who had acquired it. He was greatly upset. He decided to come East at once and straighten out the whole matter."

Jim got to his feet, went to the door. "Will you come in, please, Mr. Freelton?"

The man who came into the room was tall and thin and gray, with a distinguished face and voice. In his hands he held carefully a package perhaps eighteen inches high.

"Are you Trevor?" he asked. He shook hands. "Where is the blackguard?" His eyes went swiftly around the table and stopped at Oliver Noonan.

"That's the man who sold me the Praxiteles bust. The gallery always had a good name in Bennett's time. But this fellow—"

"Just a minute," Noonan said quickly. "I

was only acting as an agent. I have no personal responsibility in this deal at all. I was working for—"

Chester pushed back his chair and stood up. He was shaking so violently that he had to hold on to the back of his chair. His face was twitching.

"All right," he said hoarsely. "You've got me. Only let's stop talking about it! Arrest me and let's get it over with."

Noonan's lips parted. "But—"

"Come on!" Chester said sharply. "Let's go."

"Let Mr. Noonan finish what he has to say," Jim suggested quietly. Again the look he gave Chester was filled with compassion.

"I don't know what this guy is trying to do," Noonan said, puzzled. "So far as I know, he hadn't anything to do with the whole setup. The man who planned this raid on the Bellamy Institute is—was—my boss. The owner of the gallery where I work. William Bennett."

XXV

In the director's room, behind closed doors, William Bennett now sat alone with a copy of the catalogue beside him, making a list of his sales and his substitutions. The money would be returned. It was all in a couple of safety deposit boxes in New York.

After Noonan's dramatic disclosure, the meeting had been stormy. Over Roger Clayton's protests Jill refused firmly to prosecute. Publicity, arrest, a trial would only hurt the Institute further. Anyhow, Mr. Bennett was going to make full restitution.

"But the man deliberately tried to kill you," Clayton exclaimed.

Bennett sat stonily silent. It was Chester who covered his face with his hands.

"He didn't succeed," Jill pointed out. She could not look at William Bennett, the jovial man who had treated her with such apparent kindness and yet had tried, over and over, to remove her from his path, as casually as though she had been an insect, to prevent exposure.

She turned to Chester. "I believe you must have known all the time."

He raised his tortured face. It was hard to look at his naked suffering. There was compassion in the look Clayton gave him. Allen watched him with a look of surprise, a growing understanding and respect. Not once had the son looked at his father.

"I always knew," he said flatly, "that he was crooked. He can't seem to help it. That's why I wouldn't go into business with him. How he escaped exposure in the past I can't imagine, though of course he was always careful not to palm off his copies on experts. But he's my father. I couldn't expose him. And yet I couldn't stand back and let him— hurt Jill.

"At first, I didn't suspect that there was any plan to—injure you, Jill. I never dreamed of that. When the gas was turned on in your room I thought you'd done it yourself accidentally. Then—Dad said your mother was insane. You imagined things. But the car brakes—I got to thinking. I—" dark color spread over his ghastly face—"thought if you

313

married me you'd be safe. He wouldn't do anything to you if we were married. Because the Bellamy money would be in the family. But you couldn't see it that way and I don't blame you.

"Then when you told about the man at the warehouse, I went there to find out what it was all about. There was always the chance that someone else was behind this—mess. But that missing bust gave me the tip-off. I didn't know about Noonan, of course. I never went near the New York gallery after I first began to figure out what Dad was doing there.

"Well, I knew by what you had said that someone would be going to the warehouse to see whether anything had been left behind to give them away. I wanted to get there first. I saw the boxes, stole a pick-up truck and took them away. I tried to get into that upstairs room but I couldn't open the padlock. So I burned the place down. I was afraid of what might be found there."

He looked at Jim Trevor once, looked away. "I thought you—the man I heard in the warehouse—would be Dad's accomplice. But I didn't mean you to burn."

Jim's smile was warm. "I know you didn't. And I knew that the man who set the fire must be innocent of the thefts at the Institute."

"How?" Chester asked, surprised.

Jim grinned. "If you had had a key to that padlock, you wouldn't have needed to set the fire."

All this time Bennett sat unmoving, making no comment, providing no defense. But as he heard his son's tortured voice, became aware of his steadfast loyalty, even while he had tried to protect Jill, color drained away from his face. He didn't need any other punishment, Jill thought.

And then he proved her mistaken. "My own son," he said, and in his voice was the rage Jill had heard the morning he had the heart attack. "Working against me. From the beginning. If you'd gone into the business with me, as I wanted, I wouldn't have needed to call on an outsider like Noonan, though I will say he's a fine copyist, the best I know. But you quarreled with me, let me know you suspected me and that you intended to stop me. You caused my heart attack. I was help-less."

Jill listened, appalled, to the father's bitter attack on his son, who had tried to sacrifice himself for him.

"I couldn't telephone," Bennett went on. "I

315

didn't even dare send out a letter for fear you'd see it, and I couldn't get out of the house to mail it myself. So I had to give Jill that note for Noonan, taking a chance, of course, but hoping against hope she wouldn't recognize him. You did this, Chester. I wish you'd never been born!"

It was Abraham Allen who laid down the terms. William Bennett was to make full restitution and was to resign as governor of the Institute.

"You're a lucky man, Bennett," he said, "that your future rests on the decision of Miss Bellamy, who cares more about human kindness than about vengeance."

They left Bennett at his task and trooped out of the director's room.

"If you don't need me any longer," Chester began thickly, "I'd like to go."

"It's all right," Clayton told him. "You're through here. There won't be any repercussions. And don't blame yourself, my boy. You've been loyal all along the line."

"What am I going to tell my mother?" Chester groaned. "The shock of it—the shame of it—"

"Why must you tell her anything, Chester?" Jill said impulsively. "Your father will be home as soon as—he has finished here. Just tell her he is resigning because of ill health." She took a swift look around. "There is no one here who will ever make a single statement that could possibly cause her —or you—embarrassment."

"You're very generous," he choked. "Jill, will you—come back to the house?"

"No," she said quickly. "I'm sorry, Chester, but I can't go back there. Except to pack. I can't live in—his house again."

"Come home with me," Clayton said heartily. "Denise and I would be delighted to have you."

Aware of her hesitation, her reluctance, Miss Pritchard pleaded, "Can't I have her for the next few months, until she is of age? I'd love to have her with me."

Jill's face lighted up in relief. "Oh, that would be perfect!"

The two governors exchanged questioning glances and nodded.

"Then you can pack and return to New York with me today," Miss Pritchard said in delight.

"No, I can't," Jill said. "Tomorrow is the Fourth. Tomorrow night, we're holding the first meeting here at the Institute of the Good Citizens League. I must stay for that."

Jim opened the door for the two women.

"I'm glad you're not going back to New York just yet."

"But it's all over," Jill told him. "Thanks to you."

"There's still some unfinished business," he told her quietly. "After tomorrow we'll be able to take it up."

Jill returned to the Bennett house to pack, grateful that Mrs. Bennett had gone shopping and was away at the time. Then she and Miss Pritchard spent the night at Sally Meam's house. Jill poured out the whole story.

"So that's it," Mrs. Meam said at last. "Jim came to see me the day he reached Mapleville and said he was calling himself Peter Carr for the summer. I didn't like it one bit. Say what he would, I felt sure he'd do anything just to be near Denise Clayton again. Then you came here with him and—to be honest, child, you looked like a youngster seeing its first Christmas tree. Those Trevor men! They have a way with women. Seems like they can't help it. I could have told that Lola she was wasting her time. Jim never looked at any girl but Denise. Men are pretty stupid about girls like her. Time you went to bed, child. You look mighty white and down at the mouth."

Jill cried herself to sleep. She explained

318

her tears to herself by William Bennett's dishonor, Chester's humiliation and desolation, the fact that Jim, too, was the son of a man tainted with dishonor. And then she slept long and heavily from sheer exhaustion and the release from her terrible strain.

Miss Pritchard, watching her at Mrs. Meam's breakfast table next morning, envied the resilience of youth. The girl was rested, eager, glowing once more with hope.

The first shock, in what was to be a day of surprises, came with a telephone call. It was Hector Masters. One of his children was being rushed to the hospital for a critical operation. It would be impossible for him to keep his appointment in Mapleville.

Jill put down the telephone. "This," she declared dramatically, "is the end." She repeated Mr. Masters's message.

"Why," Miss Pritchard suggested thoughtfully, "don't you talk to Mr. Loomis? I wouldn't be surprised if, between you, you can convince Mr. Allen that it would be a sound idea for him to pinch-hit."

Jill squealed with delight and hugged her. "Will do. Come with me. I want you to see Mapleville, really know what it is like. Because someday I'm going to make my home here."

"Home," Miss Pritchard said. "It's your favorite word, isn't it? You've always had a special tone of voice for that word."

They drove to the little red-brick office of the *Gazette*. Loomis was busy, talking eagerly to a tall man in his middle fifties. He broke off when he saw Jill; the other man stood up. The two men shook hands warmly.

"Later then, Ted," the stranger said.

"Sure. Grand to have you back," the editor replied cordially.

The stranger turned, a handsome man with a vital face. He was unknown to Jill and yet there was something vaguely familiar about him.

When he had gone, she told Mr. Loomis about Mr. Masters's inability to fill his engagement.

"I was afraid something would come unstuck," the editor said gloomily. "This is going to spoil everything."

"Then let's ask Mr. Allen instead. He'd love it. And you can give him a real build-up when you introduce him. After all, he has earned it. He's been a leading citizen."

"Allen! Tonight? Build him up publicly just when —" Loomis broke off. "No, gal, that's out."

"Please," she begged him.

Loomis shrugged. "I'll ask him," he said grudgingly, "if you're so set on it. After all, this is your clambake. But I'm darned if I'll do anything to help the political career of that—that—" Polite words failed him. He sputtered.

He reached for the telephone, dialed a number. "Allen? . . . Loomis at the *Gazette* . . . What's that? . . . No, I don't want a story about the Institute. Why? Anything new? . . . No, I haven't heard any rumors. Point is this. We are holding the first meeting of the Good Citizens League at the Institute tonight. Hector Masters was going to deliver the principal address, get us off to a good start. Well, he's had to cancel at the last minute for personal reasons . . . Now keep your shirt on, Abe. We are *not* calling off the meeting. We —that is, Miss Bellamy wants to know if you'll be the speaker . . . Yes, it was Miss Bellamy's idea . . . All right, I'll tell her . . . Meeting starts at eight sharp. Better be there by a quarter of eight . . . Okay."

The editor put down the telephone. "Mr. Allen," he told Jill dryly, "greatly appreciates Miss Bellamy's flattering invitation.

"Still," he chuckled, "maybe Honest Abe isn't going to be so pleased about speaking tonight. Maybe he's not going to be pleased at all.''

"Mr. Loomis," Jill said in alarm, "what are you up to? What are you going to do?"

''Unfinished business,'' he told her laconically, and she remembered Jim Trevor saying *unfinished business*. "And I'm not going to introduce Honest Abe."

"But you'll have to," she protested in dismay. "You'll simply have to. There is no one else who is equipped to do it."

He chuckled. "I've got someone for that job. Sort of a deputy." He chuckled again, rubbing his hands together exuberantly. "To think I should live to see this day!"

Jill and Miss Pritchard drove around town, skipped lunch, and had one of Aunt Sally's "high" teas with sandwiches and delectable little cakes so they did not have to bother with dinner before the meeting. Jill chose a sleeveless turquoise silk dress and brushed her auburn hair until it shone. Miss Pritchard, in sheer black linen with a short white cape, was as smart as always. It was only seven-thirty when they reached the Institute, but already there were few parking spaces left. The sky was still light and the Institute with its graceful pillars glowed like a jewel in its green setting.

Jill took a long breath. "All right," she said, "let's go." They went into the directors' room. Through the open door they could hear voices from the main room, people greeting each other, settling themselves in their chairs.

"I hope there will be a big crowd," Jill said, moving around restlessly. "I do want this to be a smashing success."

"It will be," Miss Pritchard said soothingly.

"But what did Mr. Loomis mean about 'unfinished business'?"

"We'll find out soon enough. Do try to relax and not worry any more."

"I wish Mr. Loomis would come. And Mr. Allen. It's nearly time to start."

Miss Pritchard laughed softly. "You're like a pea on a hot griddle."

There was a sound in the doorway and Jim Trevor came in, dressed in summer whites, severely handsome. Severe? There was a curious grimness about him. He gave Jill a questioning look, an oddly uncertain look as though not sure of his reception. It was the first time they had met since the scene of the day before, the first real opportunity to talk since she had found him with Denise in his arms.

"Miss Pritchard," Jill said gaily, "I think you already know Mr. Trevor."

"And how much we owe you," Miss Pritchard said warmly.

Abraham Allen came in. He was transformed, beaming with good will. He shook hands heartily with Jill and Miss Pritchard.

"This was a fine idea of yours, Miss Bellamy, calling the village people together. I believe I have some concrete suggestions to make, some plans that could do a lot to improve conditions here. It was—" he hesitated and went on with an effort—"kind of you to suggest that I be the principal speaker tonight. I've given you small reason in the past to feel any particular good will toward me."

He was about to speak again when Ted Loomis came in with the tall man who had been in his office. The color drained out of Allen's face. He stared at the stranger in shocked disbelief.

"Dad!" Jim exclaimed, and Jill caught her breath, seeing now the resemblance which had puzzled her earlier.

Andrew Trevor smiled. "Hello there, son. I hear you've been doing quite a job. Your boss seems to be mighty pleased with you."

"My boss?" Jim was bewildered.

"Garrison. Old friend of mine. We've kept in touch with each other."

"Well, I'll be darned!" Jim grinned.

Jim was about to introduce his father to the two women when Abraham Allen came forward. For a moment he and Andrew Trevor looked at each other. Jill held her breath.

"I—" The words seemed to stick in Allen's throat. He saw the look of triumph on Ted Loomis's face. "I—there's not much point in my staying here, is there? By the time Loomis gets through with me—"

"How right you are," the editor said through set teeth.

"No," Jill protested, surprised at herself, because everything in her sided with the Trevors, father and son. "Mr. Allen is my guest tonight."

Jim looked at her. His face changed. He moved to his father's side and spoke quietly. His father nodded.

"Time to start," Loomis said. He led the way out to the platform which had been set up. Abraham Allen followed, looking like a man who was going to his execution.

Jill, Miss Pritchard and Jim Trevor slipped into the seats that Joe Deakam had kept for them in the front row. Every other seat was occupied. People were standing in the back of the room. As Andrew Trevor was recognized, walking onto the platform behind the other two men, there was an excited murmur of whispered voices: "That's Trevor . . . He's come back . . . What's Andy doing on the same platform as Honest Abe?"

Mr. Loomis got up slowly, stood with one hand on the high reading desk. "Fellow citizens," he began in an informal easy tone, "we've met here on a day which all Americans love, a day whose history makes us proud. We've come to talk over our common problems, to turn over ideas, to find ways to help our community and help each other."

He looked around the crowded room. "Thomas Bellamy gave the people of Mapleville this Institute with all the beauty it contains. His daughter, Miss Gillian Bellamy, has offered its use so we can meet and work together. In fact, this group itself is a result of her dream of a happier and more beautiful Mapleville."

There was a scattering of applause.

"Now," the editor's voice changed, "I am going to present to you a man whom most of you know, who was long regarded as the benefactor of Mapleville. As many of you are aware," he grinned, "Andrew Trevor had a sight more sense about civic welfare than he had about oil stocks."

There was a collective gasp.

"Andy," Loomis went on easily, as though he were chatting over the back fence instead of having launched a bombshell, "darned near lost his shirt in oil. In fact," he chuckled, "he was so carried away he had most of us losing our shirts, too."

There was an uneasy stir. What was Loomis trying to do? Andrew Trevor's expression was calm. Jill stole a look at Jim. There was a light in his face. It must be all right.

"But you can't keep a good man down," Loomis said. "Darned if Andrew Trevor didn't recoup his losses, and darned if he didn't try to recoup ours, too. But I'll let him tell you about it. Ladies and gentlemen, your old friend and neighbor, Andrew Trevor."

There wasn't a sound from the audience. Everyone in Mapleville knew why this man had gone away. Many of them had lost money because of him. He stood facing them, quiet, poised, half smiling. Miss Pritchard reached out a cold hand and clasped Jill's convulsively. For the first time in their relationship, it was she who needed support and confidence.

Abraham Allen sat, stiff and white-faced,

looking at the wreckage of his career. Loomis smiled grimly. This was the moment of retribution he had been waiting for.

"It's my own suspicion," Andrew Trevor said in a rich deep voice that easily filled the room, "that Ted Loomis hauled me up here because he's one of those loyal friends who can't rest until he gets things cleared up. He's just pointed out — very politely for him —" there was a ripple of laughter "— that I came an awful cropper a few years ago. Worse than that, I dragged a lot of my friends and neighbors into the same mess. And I think he was too polite about that."

His eyes rested on his son's face and he smiled. His smile, like his son's, transformed him.

"I'll be brief about this. All I've got to say is that it seems we've all struck gold, my friends. Or black gold, anyhow. That oil stock has paid off at last. There are a bunch of checks in the mail tonight and our accounts are, at long last, closed."

There was a wave of applause. He held up his hand.

"And now," he said briskly, "let's get on with the evening."

Abraham Allen's hands clenched, but he lifted his head, ready for the attack that was to come, that must come. But why hadn't Trevor already said that he had known of the offer to reimburse people, that he had kept still?

"My friends and neighbors," Trevor said, "for I hope that's what we are going to be again, I've taken up too much of your time. This is not my evening. It belongs to your speaker. I don't need to introduce him. No one here can fail to know what Abraham Allen has done for Mapleville."

Ted Loomis sat bolt upright, jaw dropping.

"Mr. Allen has given tirelessly of his time, he has had the best interests of this community at heart and done something about them. There is no citizen of Mapleville who has not had some reason to be grateful to him. For myself—" there was a little pause—"there is a special reason, a personal reason. Only a few short days ago, a warehouse burned down in Mapleville. My son was trapped in that burning building. Abraham Allen did everything in his power to enter that fire, to risk his own skin, to save my boy. I like brave men. I like good citizens. It is my privilege to present to you your future Senator, Abraham Allen."

The applause rose and fell; there were cheers. Abraham Allen, for the first time in his life, experienced the exhilaration of popularity. He stood looking out at the audience. Unexpectedly, tears rolled down his cheeks.

He tried to speak. Swallowed. Then he turned his back on the audience and held out his hand to Andrew Trevor. The two men shook hands silently. At last Allen turned back. He looked down at the speech he had put before him on the desk. Looked up.

"I guess," he said huskily, "this speech I've written is going to sound as if I thought I knew all the answers. I've learned tonight how little I know, how mistaken I can be. I wish you'd bear that in mind while I get through this speech."

XXVI

"Marry me, Jill. Please marry me."

Dan Holt sat on the lawn at Jill's feet. For a long time she had lain stretched out in a long chair beside the Clayton swimming pool, lost in thought. All night she had tossed restlessly, unable to sleep, trying to absorb the shocks of the evening before.

The civic meeting had been a tremendous success. When it broke up, Loomis had turned to Andrew Trevor with a grin.

"You certainly took me by surprise," he admitted, "the way you built up Honest Abe. I thought you were going to pin his ears back as he deserved. What happened to you?"

"It was Jim," Trevor explained. "My son told me that Allen tried to get him out of the building. I found I couldn't expose him. He's been warped all his life, poor devil, but I believe you're going to see a change in him from now on."

"Maybe," the editor said dubiously. "Anyhow, it was a princely gesture. I couldn't have done it myself. Well, I've got to run."

"Why?"

"Special edition of the *Gazette*. A report on the meeting. Allen announces candidacy for the Senate. Haven't had so much news in years, when you add all the kids hurt by shooting off firecrackers today. And—"

"What are you up to, Ted?"

"An item about the return of an old friend and neighbor. 'Andrew Trevor reopens Penn Manor.' Be seeing you." He hastened out of the Institute and in a few minutes his car lights went on and he left with the usual crashing of gears.

Clayton hurried forward to wring Trevor's hand, followed by Mrs. Meam and, it seemed to Jill, half the town.

The girl turned to find Jim, saw him standing against the wall, his face relaxed, free of strain, smiling at his father. For the first time since she had known him Jill saw him look boyish and not as though he carried a heavy load of responsibility.

Denise hurried up to slip her hand under his arm, to smile at him provocatively.

"Jim, I'm so happy about this. To know

things have worked out so wonderfully for you. I hear your father has become fabulously rich. I can't wait to have you tell me all about it, darling. After the night at Penn Manor when you kissed me like that, I knew nothing has changed between us."

Jill pushed her way frantically through the crowd. All she wanted was to escape. But Roger Clayton stopped her and introduced Andrew Trevor to her and to Miss Pritchard. Desperate as Jill was to get away, she had to wait impatiently while Trevor and Miss Pritchard talked, skipping from subject to subject, seeming to take a mutual delight in the conversation. Before they could leave, Trevor insisted that they both dine with him the next evening at Penn Manor. Mrs. Meam was going to open the house for him.

He turned his delightful smile on Jill. "But from all I hear she can't compete with Miss Bellamy. However, we'll do our best."

Miss Pritchard did not wait for Jill to answer. She accepted promptly for them both.

Before the Claytons left, Denise called to Jill, asking her to come for a swim the next day, "Of course you must go," Miss Pritchard said later over her protests. "No, my dear, we are *not* going back to New York tomorrow.

You'll keep your appointment with the Clayton girl and we'll both dine at Penn Manor."

So now Jill sat beside the Clayton pool. Denise, after welcoming her, had slipped away. Jill had seen her running up the stairs to the room over the garage where Jim was packing his things. Her throat was choked with the great lump in it. She blinked back tears.

"Wake up, sleeping beauty," Dan said. "Remember me? I'm the guy who just laid his life at your feet."

He got up and stood looking down at her. "I love you very much. If you could see your way clear just to put me on the waiting list —" He broke off because his voice was unsteady.

"Oh, Dan," she said gently, "I didn't realize — I'm so terribly sorry."

"Don't answer yet. Give me a little time to — prove myself, will you?"

"I'm sorry."

"It's that way, is it?" He put his hand over hers. "Don't look so sad. Not because of me. Merry Dan they call me. I should have known I wouldn't have a chance. But you can't stop a guy from hoping." He released her hand. "I hope he deserves you."

She was startled. "Who?"

"The best man." The door of Jim's room banged, and Denise ran down the steps, spots of color burning in her cheeks. The old amused smile returned to Dan's face. "Just because he mistook her for you in the dark, Denise built up some unfounded hopes." His smile deepened. "A dose of her own medicine ought to be good for my sweet cousin. Come on, beautiful, I'll race you to the end of the pool."

Jill laughed, jumping to her feet, and they dived in the pool together.

The swim did her good and she felt refreshed when she dressed for dinner. After a moment's hesitation, she put on the coral dress she had worn in New York. There was no special reason for the dress, but it seemed appropriate. She smiled mischievously at her reflection in the mirror. "Hypocrite," she told herself. "You are wearing it because Jim liked it."

Tonight, the iron gates of Penn Manor stood wide open, the house was a blaze of light. Trevor himself was at the door to welcome them, tall, impressive, as handsome as his son, a distinguished man. Behind him Jim stood, waiting. At the expression in his eyes, Jill's heart leaped.

Through dinner the conversation moved

gaily from subject to subject. Once Trevor broke off what he was saying to Miss Pritchard to demand of his son, "What on earth makes you grin like that? You look like the Cheshire cat."

Jim's grin broadened. "I can't get over it. I never was so surprised as when you walked into that meeting last night."

Trevor laughed. "Loomis cooked that up. We exchanged some long-distance calls and he put me in the picture. It struck me that Garrison had you in an impossible position here. Anyhow, it was high time to straighten out the losses my friends had sustained on the oil stock. And then—" He broke off.

"And then," Jim chuckled, "Loomis wanted you to show up Honest Abe."

"That was the general idea," Trevor admitted. "But somehow I'm glad it worked out as it did. If I ever saw a happy man I saw one last night when Abe heard that applause."

"It was a magnificent gesture on your part," Miss Pritchard told him. "You're a very forgiving man."

Seeing the expression on her face, Trevor's eyes widened, and then he leaned toward her, his own face glowing.

There was no reference to the meeting at the Institute, no mention of William Bennett's disgrace. The two Trevor men seemed to have decided to give the women a respite from the excitement of the past two days.

It was Jill who deliberately introduced the subject. "There's one thing I can't understand," she said. "I thought Mr. Bennett could not possibly be guilty because he had an alibi for the time when I fell in the river and again for the time when I was locked in the warehouse."

"Actually," Jim said, "he didn't. I've talked to Mr. Allen and Mr. Clayton. Bennett had just caught up with Allen at the door of the Institute that morning you nearly drowned. They had not been together. And when you thought he had gone to see Clayton, he had really had a telephone call from Noonan and he went to the warehouse."

"What hurts me most," Jill said, "is Chester. I'll never forget his face when he sat there, having to say those things about his own father."

She thought of Denise turning to Jim as soon as she knew his father had regained his fortune. "Chester has lost everything."

Jim shook his head. "He has plenty of guts. Remember, this isn't the shock to him it was to you. He's known what his father was for a long time. The exposure hurt—of course it did. But even that must be easier to bear than knowing—at least, fearing—his father was trying to—"

"Kill me," Jill said steadily.

"It strikes me," Trevor said, "that you are the forgiving one."

"Well," Jill explained, "I don't believe in the savage law of an eye for an eye. Mr. Bennett has been punished enough. He'll never again be able to run an art gallery along crooked lines. He has been exposed to his fellow governors of the Institute. He has had to make restitution. He has lost his son's respect. What would be gained by a public disgrace that would hurt Chester and serve no real purpose?"

Trevor nodded. "You are quite right, of course."

"Just the same," Miss Pritchard said quickly, her eyes snapping, "when I think of what this child has been through, of how narrowly she escaped—"

"It's all over," Jill interrupted. "Let's try to forget it. Start over. A new day."

A new day. She remembered the star-filled moment on the boat when Jim had said those words.

After dinner Trevor took them into his library. "I haven't had time yet to look

338

around, to renew my acquaintance with my old friends." His hand stroked the back of a book lovingly.

Miss Pritchard began to look at the titles. "Where on earth," she began eagerly, "did you ever find this—"

They were engrossed in each other. Jim led Jill out of the room, out of the house, across the lawn. He picked her up lightly and set her on the stone fence, looking down at the fern-fringed pool.

"What are you doing?" she began breathlessly.

He smiled. "I want to talk to you, so I put you where you can't run away. If you try to move, you're likely to slide down into that pool."

His smile faded. "I fell in love with you at first sight. And I couldn't say anything to you. I took one look and knew that you were the only woman I would ever want to marry. And I was bound hand and foot. As Garrison's representative, under a false name, in a false position, I couldn't even speak to you as myself. And until my father's name was cleared, I had no clean name to offer you.

"But I'm free now. I love you, Jill. With all my heart. I want you to be my wife, to be a part of Penn Manor forever. Will you—Juliet?"

"Jim, I—"

"Can you learn to love me?"

Her hands reached for his. "From the first moment I saw you, I knew I'd—"

"What?" he asked, his lips against her hair.

"I knew I'd come home." She raised her head and he bent to her lips.

The publishers hope that this Large Print Book has brought you pleasurable reading. Each title is designed to make the text as easy to see as possible. G. K. Hall Large Print Books are available from your library and your local bookstore. Or you can receive information on upcoming and current Large Print Books by mail and order directly from the publisher. Just send your name and address to:

G. K. Hall & Co.
70 Lincoln Street
Boston, Mass. 02111

A note on the text
Large print edition designed by
Cindy Schrom.
Composed in 18 pt English Times
on a Compugraphic Editwriter
by Don Dewsnap Publishing Services.